BOOKS BY MONICA HUGHES

Devil on my Back

MONICA HUGHES

Devil on my Back

New York **ATHENEUM** *1985*

An Argo Book

Permission to include lines from "Silver" by Walter de la Mare courtesy of The Literary Trustees of Walter de la Mare and the Society of Authors

Library of Congress Cataloging in Publication Data

Hughes, Monica.
    Devil on my back.

    "An Argo book."
    Summary: When the slaves rebel against the rigid social order imposed on the post-disaster colony by the all-controlling computer, Tomi, the son of the colony overlord barely escapes with his life to the outside, where he discovers what it is like to be free.
    [1. Science fiction] I. Title.
PZ7.H87364De 1985   [Fic]   84-21657
ISBN 0-689-31095-1

Contents

Devil on my Back

1
Dreamland

DEEP in the heart of ArcOne a microchip was activated. A circuit stimulated the brain of each sleeper. The City awoke. In Apartment Ten, North Quad, Tomi Bentt opened his eyes and stared at the ceiling, where the lights slowly strengthened to daytime intensity. What was special about today? Why did he feel like pushing his head under the pillow and going back to sleep, even though he had had the full eight hours of rest prescribed for his age group?

With an unpleasant flip of his stomach he remembered: Access Day. He sat up, now fully awake, and swung his legs to the floor. In the bathroom he smeared his head and arms with depilatory cream and stepped into the shower.

Ten minutes later, dry and oiled, his bald head shining, his student robes in precise folds about his shoulders, he entered the dining room. It was empty except for the family slave, who stood as mute as a piece of furniture by the serving table.

"What's for breakfast, Seventy-Three?"

"Eggs, Young Lord, and soy toast."

That was a good omen for the day, thought Tomi. The hens had not been laying well, something to do with the season, though how the seasons outside the Dome could affect the laying of the hens inside was something Tomi didn't bother to understand.

He waited greedily for Seventy-Three to serve him, but when the plate of scrambled eggs and toast was placed before him, his stomach did another flip-flop. He swallowed and put down his fork.

"Something is wrong, Young Lord?"

"No, it's just. . . I think I'm not hungry after all."

– Eggs contain the most perfect available protein as well as Vitamin A, calcium, riboflavin and thiamine – A familiar voice spoke inside Tomi's head. He sighed, obediently picked up his fork and forced himself to eat.

He was struggling with the last mouthful when Lord Bentt came quickly into the apartment. He had the look of a man who had already completed a good day's work. Tomi marvelled that he had never seen his father other than fully clothed and on the go. No matter how quickly he responded to the wake-up call in his brain, the Lord Bentt was ahead of him.

Tomi jumped to his feet and bowed as deeply as his fat belly would permit. "Good morning, my Lord. I hope you slept well?"

"Excellently." Lord Bentt sat at the head of the table and nodded to the slave to serve his breakfast. "You are up very promptly. No dreaming in the shower, eh?"

"It is Access Day, my Lord."

For an instant his father sat motionless. Then he nodded and reached for the dish of seasoning herbs. His face was expressionless. "Ah yes. Access Day. Well, I have no concern. You will bring honour to the House of Bentt."

"I will try, my Lord."

"You will succeed." His father glared at him from under eyebrows that slashed darkly across the pale hairless face. Bowed beneath his weight of accessed knowledge, Lord Bentt glowered up. "You *will* succeed."

"Y . . . yes, my Lord. Er . . . may I be excused?"

His mother drifted into the room as he rose from the table. He kissed her hand dutifully. She smiled faintly, her mind on women's things, probably the new fabric she was designing for the workers to weave. Her shoulders too were bowed with accessed knowledge, but useless stuff, thought Tomi, thankful he was not a woman.

He sat on the entrance bench for Seventy-Three to do up his sandals. One of the thongs had become knotted, and as

2

the slave stooped to disentangle it the shaggy hair parted and fell forward, exposing for an instant the ugly puckered scar across the back of the neck.

Tomi shuddered inwardly. Thank the Dome that hadn't happened to him. His surgically implanted socket had healed neatly with no hard scar tissue to twist or distort it.

The sandal was done up at last and Seventy-Three suddenly looked up, straight into Tomi's eyes. It gave him a shock, looking straight into the eyes of a slave. They were as human as his and quite young. He wondered who Seventy-Three had been before the implant failure had led to a slave's life.

"Good luck, Young Lord." Seventy-Three squeezed Tomi's foot, an unexpected, almost a scandalous gesture.

Good luck. As Tomi walked towards the main corridor that led to Centre and South Quad he thought about luck. Was luck all that separated him from Seventy-Three? That made Tomi the honoured only son of Lord and Lady Bentt and Seventy-Three a nameless slave? No, it must be more than that. Not just luck...

At the classroom door he met the other nine. They smiled weakly at each other. Even jovial Farfat didn't have a joke for the occasion. They stood in uneasy silence until the bowed figure of their tutor, Lord Vale, shuffled along the passage to the classroom.

"Ah!" He peered up, seeming surprised to see them. For the past seven years he had seemed surprised to see them. "There you are, boys. Bright and early, eh? Eager for the experience, ha, ha! Come in, then. Come in."

They made themselves comfortable on their couches, each with its familiar terminal. Tomi glanced across at his friends: Grog, Denn, Farfat, Matt. Each of them looked as pale as he felt. The five of us must have a celebration when today's over, he told himself firmly, and tried to concentrate on what Lord Vale was saying.

"For seven years, Young Lords, since you first came to me with your access sockets empty, I have instructed you. You

3

are now fourteen years of age and today will begin to become scholars. For seven years you have worn only your lifepak and have accessed one at a time some of the infopaks that will become a part of you. You have acquired some knowledge over these years: a week with a mathpak, a week with ancient history, a week with science. Now we have reached the most important day in your young lives: Access Day. Why is it called that... Grog?"

"Because today we gain access to *all* knowledge, my Lord," Grog burst out eagerly.

Lord Vale's face creased in a thin smile. "Today you *begin* to access all knowledge," he corrected. "You will begin by accessing and interfacing mathematics, physics, City history and English literature. Upon your ability to handle this information, to interface freely and to make linkages within your own brains..." He turned to show them the mighty weight of paks that lay upon his neck. "Upon your ability depends your future access to engineering, ancient history, philosophy. Only then will you become a full member of the Lordship of the City, freely interfacing with the entire knowledge of the human race."

Tomi rubbed his hands down the folds of his gown. His stomach heaved and he swallowed and wished he had left his breakfast uneaten in spite of the command of his lifepak. Lord Vale's voice droned on. He couldn't pay attention. His mind was jumping all over the place. His skin crawled and his palms were sticky again.

"...a tranquil mind," Lord Vale was saying. "You have practised these exercises daily for the last seven years. We will go through them once more. Relax... breathe in slowly... three... four. Hold it. Now out slowly... slowly... ten... eleven... twelve..."

From Farfat's couch came a winded gasp. Lord Vale looked up with a frown. "And again."

Tomi felt the fear drop from him. The knot in his stomach dissolved. His head became clear, his brain and will focussed. It has *nothing* to do with luck, he told himself again.

He jumped as Lord Vale's dry hand lightly touched the nape of his neck. "Stay relaxed. That's right. Good."

He felt pressure on his socket and the sudden weight of additional paks. The tension at the graft was unbearable. He gasped, managed a slow deep breath. Suddenly it *was* bearable. Three paks. Four. Another breath.

"Very good, Tomi. Relax. Make no attempt at access until I tell you."

His heart pounding furiously, Tomi lay on his side against the contoured cushions of his couch to ease the unaccustomed weight off his neck. Through half-closed eyes he could see Lord Vale move slowly around the room. Jay. Matt. Now he had reached Grog's couch. Good old Grog. Relax, you'll be all right.

It seemed to be taking Lord Vale a very long time. What was wrong?

An animal wail cut the tense silence. "I can't. I can't. Oh, it hurts. Stop it. Take them away..." The voice rose from a wail to a scream. A horrible noise. Revolting. Couldn't Lord Vale get Grog to stop?

"Security." Lord Vale's voice was a dry whisper. Within twenty seconds the door was flung open and two men in the scarlet uniforms of soldiers marched in, their TV monitors strapped to their foreheads. Three-eyes, the Young lords irreverently called them. Now Tomi was thankful for the quiet efficiency with which they removed the screaming Grog.

"But I don't want to be a slave. Don't make me... it's not fair..." The closing door cut off his screams like a knife.

In the sudden silence Tomi shuddered. Poor Grog! Bad luck. Or bad learning? To be turned into a nameless unfamilied slave for the rest of his miserable life, all memory of accessed knowledge and of being a Lord wiped out. To be a number...

Yet mixed with the horror was a warm glow that made Tomi more sure of himself than ever before: It didn't happen to *me*. I'm all right! I'm going to make it!

5

Lord Vale moved, stoop shouldered, to the front of the class. His face was smooth, schooled through fifty years of lordly discipline. "Relax. Breathe in slowly. One... two... three..." The voice droned on. Tomi was almost asleep when Lord Vale once more moved between the couches fitting infopaks into the sockets of the remaining students.

He finished and lightly clapped his hands. Tomi's eyes flew open. Farfat was grinning at him and he smiled weakly back. Good old Farfat. Not a gram of imagination in him.

"Are you ready, Young Lords? We will begin to access slowly, to accustom your nervous systems to the sudden high input of signals." He turned to his desk and tapped a command into the terminal. "Be ready to watch your screens and respond. Do *not* hurry. The master computer will give you access at the rate you demand and no faster. Do not be afraid to take your time. The City wasn't built in a day!"

They tittered dutifully at the old joke.

"Switch on your terminals, identify yourselves and begin."

Tomi tapped his identicode into the terminal. A question flashed onto the screen. "Give the value of pi to twenty places."

Twenty places? *I* don't know that! He took a shaky breath. Take your time, Lord Vale had said.

He reached out to the keyboard and began to tap out the answer. 3.14159265358979323846. I knew it. I knew it! He waited for the next question.

"When was More's Utopia first published?"

"1516." It was amazing. There was no sense of searching his memory. Whatever he wanted was there, *accessible*. Knowledge is power, a voice spoke inside his head. Where did it come from? His new paks? Or was it something he had found out for himself? He leaned forward eagerly towards the console.

Out of the corner of his eye he saw a sudden flashing movement and turned in amazement to see Farfat, at the end of the row, crouched over his terminal, his hand moving faster than human hand could possibly move.

6

At the same instant Lord Vale moved swiftly from his desk. Before he could reach him Farfat was on his feet, his hands to his head. "I am Farfat. Far... far... It is a far far better thing that I do than I have... far... the extent of the universe is fifty billion light years... whereas Newton's law expresses..."

Lord Vale reached Farfat, but was fought by hands clawing frantically at the old Lord's scraggy neck. Tomi leapt from his couch and ran to help. He couldn't believe the strength of Farfat, his eyes mad, howling like a dog.

"Denn, help!"

The two boys struggled to hold Farfat's wrists down while Lord Vale wrenched the infopaks from their socket at the back of his neck. Tomi saw his friend's eyes roll up into his head. He sagged forward into their arms as the soldiers again rushed in.

Tomi and Denn saw the limp body of their friend dragged from the room. The other six students lay rigidly on their couches, their eyes fixed on their screens, pretending not to notice the disgusting event.

"Thank you, boys. Continue with your work." Lord Vale's voice was calm.

Tomi's mouth fell open. "But..."

"Continue, Young Lords." There was a harsh warning behind the quiet command. Obediently Tomi went back to his console. Problems flashed to the screen and his fingers automatically answered them; but all he really saw was the mad glare in Farfat's eyes, all he heard was the demented howl of poor Grog.

I can't concentrate, he thought in panic and fumbled an answer. I can't... Could they throw me out now? Could I be programmed into a slave like Grog or a worker like Farfat?

His hands shook and he pressed the palms together and tried to breathe deeply, to think calmly, praying that the Lord Tutor would not notice him.

Lord Vale clapped his hands and at the sharp sound a chill of fear ran down Tomi's spine. But their tutor was actually smiling. "Well done, Young Lords. That will be sufficient for today. I will see you at the same time tomorrow. If you have any trouble within the next day let me know at once."

As they rose obediently to their feet he said quietly, "Denn, Tomi. One moment if you please."

Again the shiver of fear down the spine.

"Sit, Young Lords."

As Tomi settled on his couch he found himself staring straight into Lord Vale's eyes. They were a pale blue, with a sorrow in them from which Tomi turned his own eyes away.

"I believe you Young Lords were close friends of both Grog and Farfat. You must be feeling sad and bewildered and perhaps even angry at their failure."

Tomi's head jerked up. Did Lord Vale know everything? Perhaps that was the reason for the sadness in his eyes... but that couldn't be right. Knowledge was power and power was splendid!

"Why do we access this way if it is so easy to fail?" He blurted out. "Is it only luck that separates us Lords from soldiers or workers or even slaves? I don't understand *anything*." He stopped, close to tears.

Lord Vale smiled a faint humourless smile. "That is the first step on the path to true learning. Grog dreamed of gaining access to all knowledge. He was wrong, wrong! What I can teach you is only the beginning. You ask if it is all luck? Perhaps it is. All life is luck if you look at it one way. It is luck that *your* ancestors were part of the ArcOne team during the Disaster. It is luck that your forefathers lived safely underground through the Age of Confusion. It is luck that you were born as sons of Lords. It is all luck. Now ask yourself: is that a useful thing to know?"

"But why must we access this way?" Tomi cut into the gentle flow of words and then blushed for his rudeness. "I am sorry, my Lord. But surely there must be other ways of learning?"

8

"Of course. In the bad old days you would have sat for seven or eight hours a day for twelve years on a hard chair, while a teacher tried to implant knowledge out of books into your heads. It was an inefficient system and the knowledge acquired was spotty and incomplete. There is too much to learn and man no longer has the memory to retain it without help."

"What is 'memory'?"

"Memory is the ability to recall material stored in the brain without computer help. In the ancient days man was skilled at memorizing, but even before the Disaster it was a dying art. The result was ignorant specialists: scientists who made decisions about the future of mankind without knowledge of his previous history. Well, you know where that has brought us." He shrugged his bent shoulders. "To the Age of Confusion."

"So we must learn to access the computer directly?"

"The computer is your memory and mine. With every pak you access you become closer to the ideal of a perfect thinking being, with a balanced knowledge of history and engineering, science and philosophy. It is the only way to restore Mankind to its proper place and begin to set the world aright."

"Are *we* going to do that?"

"My goodness, no!" Lord Vale was horrified. "Even your learned father, my dear Tomi, has not achieved perfect access. There is always more to learn. But with each generation we come a little closer to being the perfect man who will be fit to inherit the Earth."

"But..." Tomi struggled with new thoughts. "Aren't the scientists and engineers and philosophers discovering new things all the time?"

"Stupid," hissed Denn. "That's what ArcOne's for. Isn't it, Lord Vale?"

"Correct. But you should not call your fellow student stupid."

Tomi wasn't paying attention. "Doesn't each Lord share his new knowledge with the computer and so with every other Lord?"

9

"Of course."

"Then each generation is going to have more and more to access. I don't see how we can ever catch up and be perfect enough to go Outside again."

Lord Vale nodded approvingly. "Good. You have hit upon an important concern. A dozen Lords are working on the problems of whether Learning is a finite or an infinite series."

Tomi's brain automatically accessed Math and Philosophy and grasped Lord Vale's meaning. "But if Learning *is* an infinite series we're never going to catch up and all the time we've spent in ArcOne will be a waste... my Lord," he added politely.

"We must hope that is not the case." The pale blue eyes were veiled by lids as wrinkled as crushed paper. The sharing was over.

"Yes, my Lord," said Tomi obediently.

"Yes, my Lord," echoed Denn.

"Well, well. You have both had a shock at the loss of two close friends. I shall prescribe a few hours in Recreation to forget all about it."

Recreation, thought Tomi in disgust. As if a chess game with the computer would be enough to drown the sound of Grog's screams or wipe away the memory of the mad glare of Farfat's eyes.

Lord Vale smiled, just as if he'd read my thoughts, Tomi thought uneasily. "You have attained Access today, Young Lords, and I think you might be considered men, fit to enjoy adult recreation. You may go to Dreamland."

He typed a command into the console. "Off with you, then. Happy dreaming!"

As they walked down the corridor Denn whispered, "I can't believe it. I thought you were going to get us into big trouble with your crazy questions. And now Dreamland! I've heard my Lord father speak of it, but I never expected that I..."

Tomi kicked at the white plastic wall. "Access to Dreamland won't make me forget Farfat, or Grog either. What does Lord Vale take us for?"

"Of course not," Denn agreed hastily. "I won't forget them either. But... well... Dreamland! Think how we'll be able to lord it over the others!"

Though he was ashamed of such selfish thoughts Tomi couldn't help agreeing, nor could he prevent the sense of excitement as they turned down the corridor that led to Dreamland. At the same time he had the uneasy feeling that he and Denn were being bribed to forget Grog's and Farfat's pain, the way a baby is bribed to stop crying with a sucrostik.

A soldier bumped into them outside the entrance to Dreamland. His eyes were misty; there was a smile on his lips. He started. "I beg your pardon, Young Lords. I did not see..."

Tomi waved away the Three-eye's apology and wondered what his dream had been like, to make the hard face as soft as melted plastic. He slipped his identicard into the slot in the door and Denn did the same. The door swung invitingly open. The boys looked at each other.

"Well?"

"Come on then."

There was thick carpet on the floor, an agreeable scent in the air and soft music. The boys looked around curiously. Through a shadowed arch a young worker entered the room. In the pink light she seemed quite pretty, with hazel eyes and a neatly shaped head; but apart from her lifepak, she wore on her neck only one thin pak. Quite brainless, poor thing, thought Tomi pityingly.

"Welcome, Young Lords," she said in a small flat voice, as if she were reading the words off a screen inside her head. "I see this is your first visit to Dreamland. Do you wish to dream together or separately?"

Tomi and Denn looked at each other.

"Together," said Denn.

"An adventure," added Tomi.

"Naturally the Young Lords would like an adventure. I can offer you adventures in the prehistoric past, in historic times, in the present or the future. In North America or Darkest

11

Africa, old Europe or the glamorous East. What is your choice?"

"Choices? I don't know..."

"I do. Denn, I've always wondered what it's *really* like Outside nowadays." He turned to the worker. "Could we have an adventure *out there?*"

"Certainly, Young Lords. An adventure in North America, present time. Come this way, please."

She led them soft-footed down a dimly lit hall and into a small room, empty except for two contoured couches. Tomi curled up on one as if to sleep.

"No, my Lord. Flat on your back. You will find your paks do not hurt your neck. Try and see."

The couch moved as he moved, in an odd unexpected way; but Tomi found that he could lie on his back, completely relaxed, with no pain from his paks at all. He felt weightless, floating and sinking at the same time.

Denn spoke from the other couch. "This is most strange. What happens now?"

"Patience, Young Lord. First I plug your lifepak into the back of the chair, so... and now yours, Young Lord. I will leave you and programme your desired dream."

"Suppose we don't like it?" Denn asked anxiously. "I mean... when we're in the middle of it. What do we do?"

The worker laughed, a tinkly flat sound. "The dream you order is the dream you get, Young Lord. There we are. Good dreamings, Young Lords." She closed the door softly and they were alone in the dim sweet smelling room.

"I say, Tomi. What if...?"

"Sssh, Denn. You'll spoil it if you keep..."

The music stopped abruptly. The dim light flared into painful brilliance and the subtle scent was displaced by the less attractive smell of rotting leaves.

"...if you keep talking." Tomi heard his own voice thin out into enormous space. There was something hard and bumpy under his back. He scrambled to his feet.

12

"Denn, where are you?" He stared through the brightness, his eyes watering. He rubbed them, blinked and looked around. He was standing ankle deep in fallen leaves among enormous trees. A hot brightness shone down on him. Could it really be the sun? Yes, that was it all right, and the blueness spread all around and above must be sky. He was actually outside the Dome. A shiver ran down his back.

Where was he? How far from the City? He ran a few paces through the trees, but all he could see were a thousand more trees. He ran in the other direction. The same. ArcOne was nowhere in sight. His heart began to pound. What was he doing alone in the wilderness, away from the comforting shelter of the Dome? He had a feeling, like a lost memory, that someone should be with him. Hadn't he just called someone's name? Farfat? Grog? No, definitely not them. Denn, that was it!

"Denn," he called again, "Where are you? DENN!"

His voice was lost among the silent trees and only silence answered him. He shivered and looked up. The sun was sinking quite rapidly. It no longer warmed the little glade where he stood, but flickered low between the trees, whose heavy trunks were slimed over with green stuff. Long shadows lay like bars across the ground. Over his head the branches stirred gently, as if the trees were breathing. It was really getting quite dark.

He couldn't stand still for ever. For want of a better choice he began to walk in the direction of the setting sun. At once the trees seemed to close in around him. He had the uncomfortable feeling that he was a stranger with no rights in this place. He began to run. The trees seemed to follow him.

He stumbled on for what seemed like hours, scrambling around prickly thickets that seemed deliberately to bar his way, crashing through knee-deep weeds and grasses that gave off a bittersweet smell as he brushed against them.

His heart pounded and each breath stabbed his chest and hurt his throat. At last he gained the crest of a hill and saw below him, as the trees parted, a wide valley. The sun sat just

13

above the rim of the far hill. In the dusk at the bottom, sparks of silver caught in the red sun. A river, thought Tomi, and suddenly realized how very hot and how unbearably thirsty he was.

Hungry too. His hands went automatically to his pockets and he looked down in surprise at the clothes he was wearing. What a sight he must look! A kind of breeches and an overcoat of some synthetic he had never seen before. It was heavy, but supple, of a brown colour and with a strange wild smell. The edges of the coat were decorated with fringes of the same stuff. There was a patch pocket on each hip. One was empty and the other held only a loop of cord that widened to a broad band at one place. It was made of the same stuff as his coat and breeches.

He pushed it back into his pocket and determined to reach the river before dark. The way became very steep and he had to cling to the trees to slow his pace and stop his feet from going out from under him. Then there were no more trees. The slope flattened to a meadowland, with the bank of the river just beyond.

He ran through the grass, glad to be rid of the great trees. From the shadows behind him came a long drawn out howl. He shivered and ran on, leaping tussocks of grass. The sound followed him, mournful and terrifying.

He slipped suddenly on pebbles, saved himself and saw that the river was at his feet. Which way to go, away from the monster? Downstream, he decided, and turned to the left and began to walk as fast as he could, his feet sliding and slipping among the stones. A pain shot up his big toe and he looked down to see that his feet were bare. Bare and dirty and calloused, with bruises on the toes where he had hit other stones at other times before his present memory of this life.

Again the sound came, nearer, as if whatever made it was prowling along the river bank alongside him, just on the other side of that great ridge of shadow that was the forest. He began to run and almost at once fell forward over a log that lay, half in the water, half on the stony beach. As he

14

caught his balance with both hands on its rough bark, he realized that it had been hollowed out to make a boat.

He leapt into it with a forward thrust that sent the dugout rocking into the smooth water of the river. It wavered for a minute and then its front end found the current. Tomi knelt on the wet bottom, his hands clutching the rough-hewn sides. He couldn't see how fast he was moving. Only the faint rocking motion told him that he was indeed being carried downstream.

The river became a shadow along whose dark path he was being drawn. The sun had long ago set and now above his head the sky was slowly pricked out with points of light that grew thicker and brighter as the last twilight was sucked into the shadow of the river.

"Stars," said Tomi aloud. "I am looking at the stars." He stared up in wonder, his hands clutching the sides of the dugout. Then he saw that one of the stars seemed to have fallen from the sky. It burned on the river bank, a small bright spark dead ahead. The dugout moved to the left and it vanished. Then it reappeared over to his right. Now he was closer he could see that of course it wasn't a star but a fire, burning brightly on the river bank.

Fire meant human beings. The loneliness he had felt in the forest surged back and he longed for the presence of another person. He must get over to the right shore before the current swept him past and out of sight. He felt around the bottom of the dugout for something to steer with, but there was nothing, only the damp wood.

He scrambled forward, rocking the log dangerously, and swept his hands forward through the water, trying to slow the log down and turn it out of the current. The pressure of the water was icy against the backs of his hands. It was almost unbearable. But the dugout was definitely slowing down and, instead of swinging over to the left as the river turned, the front end was still pointing at the bright spark. He paddled and pushed until his arms ached with cold.

There was a sudden wet crunch and the dugout cut into the

15

pebbly shore. He was jerked forward and hit his nose against wet bark. "Ow!"

He jumped out and staggered through shallow water towards the fire. It crackled welcomingly, flames shooting upward from the red heart of great logs. He fell on his knees beside it, dripping and shivering. A shadowy figure looked up from the far side.

"Hello," said Denn calmly. "I thought you'd never get here."

"Oh, am I glad to see you!" Tomi's teeth chattered. He held out frozen arms to the flames. Water dripped hissing into the heart of the fire.

"Watch out. You're dripping on our dinner."

"Dinner? Really, Denn? I'm starving! What is it?"

"Fish. I caught them myself."

"How on earth. . .?"

"In that little pool over there. It was easy. I just waded in and caught them through their gill-flaps. Then I found a sharp stone to fillet them and put them on the hot rocks to roast. They should be just about done by now."

"How did you start the fire?"

"Don't you remember ancient history? Rubbing two sticks together. Nothing to it. Here, help yourself."

Tomi burnt his fingers picking a pink piece of fish off the stone. He bit into it gingerly. "Delicious," he said with his mouth full. "Ow, burnt tongue!" He scooped cold water from the river and drank from his hand.

Never had a meal tasted as marvellous as the creamy fresh fish seasoned with wood smoke and hunger. The fire, which Denn kept fed from a pile of driftwood, sent flames and sparks crackling cheerfully into the black sky. Beyond the circle of light were the black dangers of the forest, but within it they were as safe as in a magic circle.

When every scrap of fish was finished, Denn dug into the shimmering embers with a stick and rolled out half a dozen blackened objects. "Edible roots," he said smugly. "Watch you don't burn yourself."

16

Tomi broke one open with a clean stick. An appetizing smell gushed out with the steam. He nearly dropped it, and Denn showed him how to hold it in a double layer of green leaf to protect his hand. The flesh was sweet and mealy and very satisfying. By the time he had finished two roots he couldn't eat another thing. He yawned vastly.

"Sleep first if you want to," Denn suggested. "I'll keep the fire going and wake you when I get tired."

"Hmm." Tomi curled up by the fire. The grass made a soft bed beneath him. The stars above were almost too thick to count. Ten... twenty... fortytwo... fortythree...

DENN was shaking his shoulder. The fire was a bed of dull red ash on which a couple of pieces of driftwood smouldered. The darkness was very close around them.

"It's all my fault, Tomi. I fell asleep and let the fire die down. Tomi, there's something out there and it's coming closer."

Tomi's eyes strained into the darkness. He could see nothing. "What sort of something?"

"I don't know. Horrible. There!"

A snarling spitting sound broke the silence. The whole forest seemed to gather itself together to listen. Even the river's voice quietened. In the centre of the dark two lights glowed like faint red coals. Another snarl shattered the dark. Much louder. And the twin coals were closer.

"Tomi, you've got to stop it. Now!"

"Me? I don't know how..."

"You've got the weapon. In your pocket. Oh, hurry!"

Tomi's hand was in his pocket, feeling the strip of stuff that he had discovered before. He pulled it out and let the knowledge of it flow into his fingers. He groped in the dark until his hand found what felt right, a smooth round pebble about the size of a hen's egg. He dropped it into the wide part of the band, whirled the whole thing round and round his head and with a sudden jerk freed the stone.

17

He heard the hiss of its passage through the waiting dark. There was a thud, a grunt, a heavier thud. The two red lights were no longer there. Tomi shivered and felt sick. Had he really killed it? A living thing? He wanted to throw the weapon away, out into the river, but perhaps there were other creatures still lurking in the dark.

"Get the fire going, can't you?" he said over his shoulder.

"I've put on more wood but it won't catch."

"Fan it with a leaf or something. Blow on it. Hurry, Denn."

Two more red coals appeared out of the blackness a little to the right of the last. Tomi groped for another stone. The lights came nearer, very close to the ground. They stopped. He could smell its bitter, wild animal scent. His hands shook as he slipped the stone into the sling. I don't want to kill it, whatever it is. I wish I didn't have to. . .

At the instant of his thought the fire finally caught and a great gout of flame licked up, mapping a circle of reality on the thick darkness. Within this circle Tomi could see his shadow, black against the harsh pale grass, the arm raised menacingly. In the tangle of brush at the limit of light he caught a glimpse of spotted fur, of sharp ears tufted with hair. Then there was nothing but tangled brush. The flames shrank. Reality shrank, until there was nothing at all but the patch of grass he was kneeling on. Then that too vanished and there was nothing at all.

"I HOPE you had a good dream, Young Lord." He opened his eyes and stared blankly at the young worker. She unplugged his connection to the couch and turned to Denn. Tomi sat up and swung his feet to the ground. His body felt uncomfortably fat and unwieldy and the paks dragged painfully at the nape of his neck. Funny, in the dream he had felt so supple and free. . .

"Wow!"

"Wow indeed. How do you feel?"

"Fantastic! As if I had just climbed the highest mountain or. . . or. . ."

"Discovered a new world?"

18

"Yes. Yes! Denn, weren't our bodies amazing? We could do *anything*."

The two boys shuffled out of Dreamland. The main corridor was full of students strolling towards the dining room.

"Suppertime already? That was a long dream."

"Well, it did last a day and a night. I'm starved."

"Me, too. That fish you caught was a long time ago."

Denn stopped to stare. "What do you mean: *I* caught? When I came downriver in the dugout *you* were there, cooking the fish as calm as you please."

"Huh? It was I who came downriver, Denn, and found you by the fire."

"How strange. All right then: which one of us do *you* say killed the wild beast?"

"I did, of course. You nearly let the fire out, you silly goat. That was a close squeak!"

Denn shook his head. "In my dream *you* dozed off and *I* saved us with that weapon."

They glared at each other, not noticing the bumps and complaints of the other lordlings trying to get into the dining hall. Then Denn broke the tension with a laugh.

"Now I see! The worker asked us if we wanted the same dream. That's just what we got – with each of us the hero."

"Of course. Sorry, Denn. For an instant then I actually wanted to *hit* you."

Denn threw his arm over Tomi's shoulder. "So did I. That's what comes of dreaming about the savage world out there. Let's forget it. That fish tasted wonderful, but my stomach tells me it needs real food. Come on."

"It's a pity though," said Tomi thoughtfully as they picked up their trays.

"What is?"

"I was going to ask you how under the Dome you could start a fire by rubbing two sticks together."

"Sorry, I can't help. I was wondering that too."

19

As Tomi stripped off his robe that night he found himself looking at his naked body in the mirror. Pale and fat, under-muscled, his shoulders already learning the stoop necessary to support the weight of his paks; it was not a beautiful body. He sighed, remembering that other Tomi, muscled and brown. Free. He tried to stand upright and pull his stomach in, but it was really too uncomfortable. He quickly let his body slump back to its ordinary posture. After all, the other had been but a dream.

It was only in the last few seconds before the sleep signal was activated in his brain that he remembered poor Grog and Farfat.

2
The Revolt

AT UNEXPECTED MOMENTS during the next week the memory of Dreamland returned to Tomi: the bitter smell of wet leaves, the sweet smoky taste of freshly cooked fish. How real were the products of Dreamland? Was it all made up like a story in an old-style book? Or was the wilderness outside ArcOne really like that?

One free period he did something that had never crossed his mind before: he went exploring. Impulsively he stepped into one of the central elevators and looked at the display panel. Where should he go? There were only six buttons: G. 1. 2. 3. 4. 5. He had spent his life on Three, where the inhabitants of the City lived and slept, ate and studied. Below him lay the floor where all the raw materials salvaged at the beginning of the Age of Confusion had been stored. Below that, at Level Five, were the intricacies of the water treatment plant, the recyclers, and the generator, through which the river that ran Outside was diverted to turn the turbines and make the City's electricity. The solar heat storage tanks were down there too. Boring stuff, only fit for workers and slaves.

He looked at the other buttons. On the second floor were all the factories, manned by an army of workers, people only capable of carrying one or two workpaks. Above, on the first floor, were the yeast vats, the soya synthesizers and all the other aspects of food production, both real and artificial, for the twelve thousand persons, Lords, soldiers, workers and slaves, who made up the population of ArcOne.

Ground. He had never been to the top of the City before.

Feeling very daring Tomi touched the button marked G. The TV monitor in the ceiling of the elevator swung to check his identity. Then the door slid shut and the elevator moved silently upward.

When the door sighed open Tomi stepped out into the smell of the Dreamland forest. Wild. Wet. Green. He took a deep breath and looked around. Five hundred metres away the Dome met the ground in a concrete buttress that was the outer wall of the buried city. He leaned back and tried to look up, but his paks tugged painfully at the nape of his neck and he quickly slumped back into his lordly stoop. But he had seen that the sky above the transparent Dome was not the miraculous blue of Dreamland but a dirty grey. So much for dreams!

He strolled along the path that led from the central elevator block in a southeast direction. His sandals crunched pleasantly against damp pebbles. On either side grew green vines with globular fruit, green, yellow and red. Why, they were tomatoes! How extraordinary to see a tomato growing. Beyond the tomatoes were rows of other vines with coarse furry pods. He called to a worker busy plucking the ripe pods.

"What are those things?"

"Soy beans, Young Lord. They are used for..."

"Yes, yes. I know what they are used for, better than you, I should think. I have never seen them growing before, that is all. What lies beyond there." He pointed to the curve of concrete wall, now about two hundred metres away.

The worker stared. "Why... Outside, Young Lord."

"I know that, stupid. Is it possible to see what it looks like?"

"Oh, yes. May I show the Young Lord?" The worker scurried along the pebbled path to the wall, which stood about waist high and was so deep that when Tomi reached across it he could not touch the plastic skin that was the Dome.

He stared out. He was looking down a long valley, whose steep slopes were thickly wooded with dark trees. Beyond were more hills, more valleys, vanishing into a greyness of distance. It was very still, very empty, very enormous.

22

"Some Lords are not able to look out even though they know the Dome is there," the worker said suddenly.

"I am not afraid," Tomi lied.

"I can see that, Young Lord."

Tomi looked sharply at him, but the worker's face was blank. He was dressed in trousered overalls and clogs. Now that Tomi looked at him closely he could see that his hands were covered with a network of fine scars and scratches and that the back of his hands and the top of his bald head were pink.

"Why is your skin that strange colour?"

"It is the sun, Young Lord. By the end of summer these will be brown. Have you seen all you wish, Young Lord?"

"No. Wait a minute." Tomi leaned far out across the wall. Below him was a cleft through which a twisted grey ribbon of water rushed, flecked with spots of creamy white. His eyes followed it down and to the south until it was lost among the folded hills.

"I wish to see more. Over there." Tomi pointed towards the east quad, and the worker obediently led him along a curved path around the edge of the Dome. Here the river had been constricted by concrete walls and buttresses, ending in a dam, over which it poured in a white torrent. It looked frighteningly powerful.

"That structure must channel the river into the generator down on Level Five," Tomi said aloud, awed at the skill of those early engineers who had built the City five floors deep into bedrock close to this gorge down which the river poured.

"Perhaps, Young Lord. I do not know," said the man indifferently.

"Do you ever see animals close to the Dome?" Tomi had a sudden shivering memory of the glowing eyes and the yawning snarl of his dream.

"Oh, no, Young Lord. That is not permitted. They might damage the Dome. See that fence?" He pointed to a high mesh of silver that circled the concrete pad on which the Dome stood. "That has a power to stop animals."

23

"An electric fence. Of course." Tomi felt very lordly and at ease now, standing in the warm damp of the Dome, looking at the wilderness so very safely on the other side. Looking closely at the fence he now noticed little rags and tags of bone and skin where animals had tried to reach the Dome and failed.

"It is a pity the sun is not shining. The view is very grand when the sun shines." The worker beamed as proudly as if it were *his* Dome, *his* view. Really, he was absurd.

Tomi couldn't help smiling. "You like your work here?"

The man's face glowed. "Oh, yes. It is wonderful."

"Do you not get bored with picking soybeans all day?"

"Why no, Young Lord. After all, there are also peas to pick and tomatoes and..."

"Yes, yes. I get the idea. It sounds very monotonous."

"It is important work, Young Lord. *I* pick the food *you* eat."

"So you do." Tomi laughed.

"Is there anything else you wish to see." The man fidgeted from foot to foot.

"Why? What's the matter with you all of a sudden?"

"Nothing, Young Lord. But perhaps I should mention that in three minutes and forty seconds the sprinklers will come on. Do you wish to get wet?"

Tomi glanced at the network of pipes hanging some ten metres above his head. "Of course not, stupid oaf." He jumped up. "Don't you dare start them until I get back to the elevator!"

"They are automatic, Young Lord. I suggest you hurry, if you really do not wish to get wet."

Tomi waddled along the path as fast as his fat and his loose sandals would allow. Halfway to the elevator block at the Dome's centre he looked back. The worker was still standing where Tomi had left him. Foolish fellow. He'd like to tell him off.

He had to run the last hundred metres. It was most unpleasant. His heart pounded against his chest wall and he had to lean against the elevator housing to catch his breath. His robe was quite damp. Disgusting. Before going down to the familiar comforts of Three he looked back. The vines were now a brilliant green under the gentle mist coming from the sprinklers. The air felt fresh and lively. He felt suddenly reluctant to return underground.

IN THE NEXT six weeks Tomi and his class accessed another four paks. Now, at last, he really understood the noble purpose of ArcOne: to keep civilized Man and his knowledge safe through the Age of Confusion. Once that was over they would once more go out into the world and start again. Only this time there would be no mistakes. It made one proud to be a Lord.

Day after day he acquired more knowledge, until the stoop of his shoulders almost matched that of Lord Vale himself. At the end of six months only three of the original ten in his class remained. The others had fallen out, to become soldiers or skilled technical workers. Luck or brains? Tomi wondered about it and on the last day of Access drew a sigh of relief. He'd made it to the top!

"I knew you would not let down our House," Lord Bentt said calmly.

The Lady Bentt patted her son's cheek with a soft hand. "Yes indeed. Tomi, I will design a New Lord's gown for you myself, and my women and slaves will start weaving it at once."

Even Seventy-Three congratulated him. But of course there was an honour in being the slave of one of the chief families: an honour to the House was also an honour to its slaves. Tomi nodded casually and went on thinking about the Togethering and the Feast. He never noticed the hurt expression on the slave's face.

To honour the New Lords the people of ArcOne – excluding the slaves, of course, who weren't really people – were to gather in Assembly for a Togethering, followed by a great feast for all, Lords and Ladies, soldiers and workers. This time the feast was to honour *him*. And Denn and Matt, of course, he remembered hastily.

As soon as the computer awakened him on the special day Tomi jumped out of bed. He took extra care showering, making sure that there was not a single slavish hair on his face or head or arms. He dressed in his finest undershorts and shirt and draped the new robe across his shoulders, so that the great mound of infopaks showed to advantage. His mother's design was beautiful, woven of the finest synthetic in pale blue, with a design along one selvedge of green, purple and silver that cunningly interwove the Bentt family crest, Tomi's name and the date.

He looked at himself in the mirror and admired his lordly stoop and paunch. He ran his mind lovingly over his store of knowledge. It gave him a comfortable feeling of power.

After a leisurely breakfast Lord Bentt rose and offered his arm to the Lady Bentt. Then he turned to Tomi. "Come, my son." *Son*, he said and smiled. Yes, it really was a smile. He gestured for Tomi to walk upon his other side.

Seventy-Three knelt at the door to fasten their sandals, and to whisk away imaginary dust from their ceremonial robes. Her face was tense and she went on flicking and twitching at Tomi's robe until he pushed her hand away.

"Enough! Wish me joy if you will, but stop fussing."

"Take care, my Young Lord."

Take care. What an odd well-wishing, Tomi thought, but then forgot about it as they joined the crowds outside. The South Quad was already thronged with eager holidaymakers, and the Assembly was almost full as they made their entrance. Had Father planned it so?

The seats of the Lords, covered in pale blue, circled the central dais. Behind them were ringed the red seats of the soldiers, and behind them rank on rank of brown seats where the workers crowded and jostled, eagerly whispering together. It hummed like a hive. Of the twelve thousand inhabitants of the City nearly ten thousand were present to watch the formal Lording of Tomi Bentt! And Matt and Denn, he reminded himself.

The Bentts settled in their accustomed seats in the front circle facing the stone block on the dais that centred the room. Slowly the lights dimmed. Voices hushed into silence. The blue flame that hovered above the altar grew until it was as high as a man. As high as a tree.

"You are a vital part of the City." A voice spoke softly inside Tomi's head. He could never remember afterwards if it had been a man's voice or a woman's. He only remembered that it was gentle and firm and he could have listened to it for ever.

"You are part of the Great Experiment of ArcOne. Without you the City would be the poorer. Without your thought, your research, your sharing of gifts the Experiment will fail. ArcOne thanks you for your life, your work, your dedication..."

The voice went on and on. Afterwards Tomi could not remember exactly what it had said. It was more as if he had been listening to some great music that left him feeling stronger, happier, prouder than ever to be an important part of ArcOne.

After a long time the voice died away. The flame quivered and slowly shrank. There was a universal sigh of parting sorrow. Then the lights went up and everyone sat up and blinked, looked at each other, smiled, shared their happiness. To be part of ArcOne, to share the burden and the greatness, was almost too much to bear.

Tomi saw many of the soldiers shaking hands, slapping each other on the back, while the more emotional workers openly wept as they hugged each other. The flame had spoken to them all, he realised, but in different words, perhaps with a different voice.

A scream shattered the joy. Everyone shuddered, drew back and then turned to the big doors from where the sound had come. A few people moved towards the door and then suddenly shrank back.

Down the main aisle ran a woman in everyday worker's clothes, her apron half off, splattered red. Her hand was pressed to her side as though she had been running for a long time. In the stunned silence her laboured breathing was harsh. She clung to the rough-hewn stone of the altar.

"The slaves..." Her voice faded. She pulled herself erect and spoke again. "The slaves are in revolt. They have killed my man!" Her hands flew above her head in a gesture of despair, and everyone saw her left hand red with blood, blood flowing from her side. She slid down against the altar, leaving a smear of red on the white stone.

Ten thousand people began to talk at once, each voice raised to compete with the other nine thousand nine hundred and ninety-nine. Lord Bentt slipped quickly from his place to stand on the central dais. Tomi saw his lips move, but he could not have been trying to talk to the crowd. They could not possibly hear.

Yet now within his head was a voice – was it the same voice that had spoken out of the flame? – telling him to sit quietly and relax, that all would be well, that the problem would be taken care of. Around him the room stilled.

My father has *that* much power, Tomi thought with an odd mixture of fear and elation. Then into his mind jumped the even more terrifying knowledge: some day that power will be *mine*. Why did I think that? Did the Computer tell me or am I crazy? His heart beat furiously.

Now Lord Bentt was ordering the soldiers to switch on their head monitors and check the state of each floor of the City. One soldier stood to report. "They occupy much of this floor and part of manufacturing and food preparation..."

"If they destroy the vats we will all starve," muttered a blue-robed Lord.

"What about the generator? That is an even greater danger."

"There is no one down there except the designated workers and the muck-shovellers," reported the soldier. "What strategists!" Some of the soldiers sniggered.

Lord Bentt looked at them cold-eyed. "Do not underestimate their anger, soldiers. Send two units up to One and Two to regain control. One unit to man all elevators. The rest cover this floor. Off with you!"

The soldiers filed quietly from the room.

"Now, workers, to your apartments, Keep your families together and open your doors to no one until you are given permission. Lords, we will set up a monitor map on the computer and develop our best strategy. Come."

Tomi got to his feet. His father caught the movement. Again a faint smile twitched the corner of his mouth. He raised a hand. "Students, both Young Lords and New Lords alike... to your apartments!"

"But... my Lord."

"Tomi, you will do my bidding *now*."

Pouting, Tomi joined the crowd struggling to move from the Assembly Room to the living quads. Most of the workers lived on the outer arcs of East and North Quad. Tomi found himself swept along with the crowd, unable to wriggle free and get to the safety of his home on the first arc of North Quad. He was squeezed between well-muscled bodies, considerably taller than himself.

"Help. Let me out! I am Lord Tomi!" But they paid no attention, intent only on getting safely home themselves.

By the time the crowd had thinned enough for Tomi to wriggle to one side and flatten himself against a wall, he found he had been carried far along the main eastern corridor that ran from Circle Four out to Circle Fourteen. He was about as far from home as it was possible to be.

He watched apartment doors open and slam shut, mothers dragging reluctant children, grandparents being helped along. Soon all the doors were shut and there was nobody. Except him.

His heart pounded and he told himself firmly that there was nothing to worry about. The soldiers would keep an eye on him on their monitors. He walked slowly back towards Centre, his sandalled feet making a light lap-lapping on the

29

plastic floor. To left and right, passages curved away. Ten. Nine. Eight. Seven. He made up his mind that when he got to Four he would turn right and take a short cut across to the main Northeast corridor. From there it was only three blocks to Centre. He would ask for help if there was any trouble. After all he was a Lord now.

The passages of the Third Floor of ArcOne were like a spider's web radiating from the centre where the elevators stood. The design was as familiar to Tomi as the lines on the palm of his hand. Only now, as he imagined slaves armed with knives ready to spring on him around the next curve, the familiar web felt like a trap.

Once the lights dimmed and he pressed himself against a wall. Suppose he had to find his way home in the dark? But they strengthened again and he went on, almost running, determined to reach the safety of home before they dimmed again. His fat belly wobbled. He was hot and out of breath.

His panic speed was his undoing. He turned right into the curve of the fourth passage and ran smack into a person. No, three people. He saw the tangled hair, the short tunics and the bare feet of slaves. He tried to turn and run back.

"Not so fast, Young Lord." His arms were twisted cruelly behind his back. He screamed before he could stop himself.

"What have we here?" One of them pulled the edge of his toga so as to bring the design closer to his eyes. His lips moved. "Well, well, here's a pretty prize!"

"Come on, stop messing about. Kill him and let's get on."

"Hold on, blockhead. D'you know who this brat is? He's the New Lordling, son of the high and mighty kiss-your-hand Lord Bentt, that's who he is. Listen to me, my dears. We're not going to lay a hand on him. He's for Twenty-Four. Twenty-Four will know what to do with him. Where *is* Twenty-Four?"

"In the workers' dining hall."

"Off we go then. He *will* be pleased."

They dragged Tomi along the passage. As they turned into the wide corridor that ran straight from Centre to the Northeast rim, Tomi yelled. "Security! Soldiers, help!"

"Save your breath. They won't hear. Or see either." The slave walking ahead gestured to the ceiling where the TV monitor dangled uselessly by its wires.

But the soldiers have the elevators, Tomi reminded himself. That was one of the first things Father had told them to do.

Sure enough, they were there, a solid red presence, backs to the elevator doors, stun guns raised. "Help!" Tomi yelled again.

The slave who had been in front stepped quickly to one side. The ones who had been holding Tomi pushed him forward. Their thin fingers bit painfully into his fat arms. He wanted to cry. It was all so unfair. This was to have been his special day and these slaves had turned it into a nightmare. Something cold and sharp was pressed lightly against his bare throat.

"Better not move, Little Lord, or you'll lose more than your dignity."

He stood quivering. He recognised one of the soldiers across the concourse. "*Do* something," he wailed, but the man's face was blank with shock. There was obviously nothing in his fighting pak to tell him how to cope with this situation.

"Listen, soldiers," said the slave who seemed to be the leader of the three. "Unless you want to see the blood of the New Lord of Bentt trickling at your feet you'd better start moving. Around to the right there. Yes, all of you. Down the Southeast corridor. Go on. Hurry it. To passage Five. Now out of sight. I don't want a sight of red anywhere."

As soon as the soldiers had vanished, the three slaves dragged Tomi around the concourse to the next bank of elevators and the next group of soldiers.

"Help me!" screamed Tomi, and the men sprang forward, only to freeze when they saw the knife at Tomi's throat.

31

Again they were forced to retreat up the corridor and out of sight.

Tomi was pushed along the Southwest corridor to the workers' dining hall. An elaborate pattern of knocks on the door was answered by the scraping of a bolt. The door was opened cautiously and Tomi was whisked inside.

"Where's Twenty-Four? Got a nice surprise for him."

"Over there, talking to the committee."

"Right. Come on, Lordling. March!"

He was pushed down the room to a table where eight slaves sat talking. Now the knife was no longer at his throat he felt much braver. "Who is responsible for this outrage?" he spluttered, wishing his voice were deeper and more commanding. But anyway I am a Lord, he told himself firmly, and stared at the seated men.

The slave at the head of the table stared back at Tomi as if he were some kind of loathsome freak. Tomi had never been stared at by any slave before, never looked at as if he were horrible. He tried to stare boldly back, but felt his eyes wavering and his cheeks growing hot.

The man said nothing, but began to play with a knife that had been lying on the table. He held it in his right hand and ran the fingers of his left hand along the flat of the blade. Then he flipped the knife so that it flew into his left hand. And again. The blade caught the light each time he tossed it. Tomi couldn't take his eyes off that flash... flash... He swallowed and prayed he wasn't going to faint. He hadn't believed that slaves could actually *hate*.

"So you think this fat fledgling could be useful, Eighty-Seven? Why?"

"He's the New Lord of Bentt, that's why."

"Bentt!" The knife suddenly plunged into the table and stayed there, quivering. Tomi's knees sagged and his captors hauled him upright, hard hands under his armpits.

Then Twenty-four laughed. He smacked his hand on the table and pulled the knife free. "Well, why not? It's worth a try, Eighty-Seven, though I think you overestimate the

32

power of fatherly love. Don't you know that ice water flows in the veins of the Lord Bentt?"

"Let's open the young 'un's veins and see if they're the same." A slave sprawled at the foot of the table suddenly spoke.

"Fool! Hands off or we'll have nothing to bargain with. You've done well, Eighty-Seven. See the Lordling is tied up good and tight and tucked away in a corner of the kitchen out of harm's way."

Tomi was dragged across the huge dining hall to the kitchens beyond. Here his hands were tied behind his back and the end of the cord looped around the leg of one of the massive kitchen tables. The door swung shut and he was alone.

Tomi crouched against the table leg and wept. Life just wasn't fair. If they hadn't recognized him as his father's son they would never have bothered with him. If Mother hadn't had the fanciful idea of weaving the family crest into his new gown they wouldn't have recognized him. If those stupid workers hadn't pushed him in the wrong direction in their panic to get home, he would be safe in the family apartment. If...

His stomach rumbled. Not even dinner. At the thought of the great feast cooling on its dishes in the Lords' Hall, *his* feast, his celebration, he wept more bitterly than ever. The smell coming from the pots on the stove close by, inferior though it must be to the food he was accustomed to, became more and more tantalizing as the hours dragged by.

After a long time the appetizing smell turned to one of burning food. Later on a slave came into the kitchen, sniffed the air, cursed and turned off the burners on the big stoves. He left without paying any attention to the New Lord Bentt, sniffling against a table leg.

More time went by. A need even more pressing than hunger attacked Tomi. He yelled and went on yelling until a slave poked his head around the corner of the door. "Shut your face, Lordling, or we'll shut it for you."

"But I have to go to the bathroom."

"Then go." The door slammed shut. Tomi closed his eyes and moaned.

He opened them at the sound of a faint shuffling. A slave slid into the kitchen, not swaggering with head up, as the others had done, but softly, eyes downcast, the way slaves were supposed to move. She pushed her tangled hair out of her eyes.

"Seventy-Three!"

"Hush! Oh, be quiet, Young Lord." She stood above him, her hands twisting together, an expression in her eyes that he did not understand at all. "Oh, *why* did it have to be you? Any of the other Lordlings, I would have cheered whatever they did."

He stared up at her, not understanding. "You've got to help me, Seventy-Three. Untie me. I'll tell Father to give you anything you..."

She drew back and stood upright. "You don't know anything, do you? All that knowledge on your back and you don't know the simplest..." She began to laugh softly, her hand to her mouth. Then she seemed to recollect, looked anxiously over her shoulder and knelt beside him, working away at the knots, which had tightened in Tomi's useless struggles.

"There. That's it. Now you've got to hide and stay hidden until it's all over. There's nothing more I can do. They'd kill me if they knew."

"But where? If they see I'm gone they'll search everywhere for me." He stood with a gasp, clutching at the table, and stared wildly round at the row of sinks, the high tables, the ovens, the array of pots hanging from the ceiling. "There's nowhere..."

"The garbage chute!" Seventy-Three pointed to the wall, where Tomi could see a square hole liberally spattered with old gravy and other unrecognisable leftovers. It was covered with a flap that swung loosely from above.

"Garbage?" Tomi drew back.

"Oh, you great stupid! Don't you understand? They'll kill you in a minute if your father doesn't give them everything they want. And you know the Lord Bentt will never give way, not even to save you."

"But..."

"Come on. Climb through. There's a kind of ridge on the inside you should be able to stand on. I know, I worked in the kitchen once, and it was always hard to clean in there. Listen carefully, Young Lord. Hold on tight whatever happens, because it's a straight drop down to the main sewer."

As Tomi hesitated beside the gravy-encrusted opening, she gave him a little push and then ran from the kitchen like a shadow.

Death or a garbage chute? Tomi gulped. He consulted his lifepak and then all the infopaks he had acquired so painfully in the last six months. They gave him no useful suggestion at all.

For the first time in his adult life he made up his own mind. He wound his new gown closely around his middle and tucked the loose end tightly so it would not get in his way. He pushed up the flap. A stink of rotted vegetables and ancient grease hit him in the face. He gulped again, turned and scrambled feet first through the hole. His toes scrabbled wildly. Where...? Yes, there was the ridge, almost a shelf, about a metre down, probably the end of a flooring joist. He squatted with his fingers hooked over the lower edge of the chute opening.

The joist was slippery with grease. The smell was even stronger now he was on the inside. He was in darkness, except for a thread of light from the sides of the not-quite-shut flap. A very long way below he could hear the sound of running water.

Tomi crouched in the stinking darkness for what seemed like hours. After a while his thigh muscles became an agony of red-hot cramps. Bearing that pain without screaming out loud took a lot of his attention. Now and then he whimpered softly.

35

Suddenly the door was thrown open with a crash that echoed around the huge kitchen. Tomi jumped and almost slipped from his greasy perch. He heard running feet and the confused sound of many voices. Had they come for him? And what would they do when they found him missing?

Very cautiously he raised himself a few centimetres so that he could peer through the tiny slit between the frame and the flap of the garbage chute. The kitchen was full of slaves. The nearest stood so close to him that he could have reached out and touched the man's coarse tunic. They all held knives, and the faces of those he could see were full of fear and anger.

Tomi shrank down. What was happening? Were the slaves winning, or was this their final retreat?

Almost immediately his question was answered. A powerful voice echoed through the kitchen. "Ahoy. We know you're in there. Resistance is useless. Drop your weapons and come out one by one with your hands up. You will not be harmed if you obey."

A jeering laugh greeted this last remark.

"Why don't you come and make us?" A voice suggested. There was a chorus of agreement. Then silence. Unbearable silence. What was going on?

Slowly Tomi hauled his fat body up to take another look. The slaves stood alert, their eyes on the door. The knives looked wickedly sharp.

I should warn the soldiers, thought Tomi. But if I do they'll haul me out and cut my throat. I'd better be quiet. After all, they're trained to know what to do. He waited tensely. His heart was beating so loudly it was amazing that the slave standing close to the chute didn't hear it.

A woman's voice cried out in fear. A hand pointed at the air exchange grille above the stoves. The slaves crowded back. Tomi could see a faint greenish mist drifting across the room and slowly settling on the floor.

Sleeping gas! Good for the soldiers. In a minute the whole rebel gang would drop to the floor and he could climb out. A shower! A meal!

36

An intense sweetness filled his nose and mouth, blotting out the smell of rotting vegetables and sour grease.

Oh, no! He tried to hold his breath. His eyes felt as if they would pop out of his head. He couldn't possibly go on holding it long enough. Desperately he pushed up the flap and threw his body through the opening. His fat stomach caught the bottom of the frame, he gasped, inhaled and slowly sagged. He had a foggy glimpse of the kitchen, slaves staggering, falling, prone on the floor. His armpits caught on the frame for a second, but the weight of his body pulled him down.

"Help...!"

He fell, the way you fall in a dream, for an incredible distance. Then he was vaguely aware of a jolting blow to his legs. He was sliding rolling falling very fast along a wet slope. The noise was overwhelming. Crashes, echoes, pounding water. It was absolutely dark.

With a shock he was hurled into a world of brilliant white. He was flying – no, he was falling again – through the air. Then a white mass as hard as concrete rose up and smacked the wind out of him. He was struggling in icy water. Under water, greenish grey. Up again. Choke. Gasp. His hands and legs were making feeble pawing movements through the water. He saw brilliant light again, gasped for air and choked. A wave slapped into his open mouth and he went under.

3
The River

THE WILD water pounded Tomi under and as suddenly released him. He popped to the surface coughing and wheezing. This time he was able to force a tiny thread of air into his sodden lungs before he was slapped under. His arms and legs moved desperately to regain the surface. One leg struck something hard and painful. The same something nudged his side and he flung himself at it, clutching it with both hands. He got one leg across it, heaved himself up and lay with his cheek pressed against rough wetness. He brought up the water he had swallowed and lay and groaned.

Whatever had saved him was little better than what he had had before. It bobbed and pitched, rolled and shuddered and twisted as if it wanted to get rid of him. He clung to it with elbows and knees and fingernails. With his eyes tightly shut he concentrated on learning how to breathe again. He coughed until his eyes and nose ran and then threw up again. The water slapped over his face and washed it clean.

Slowly he became aware of the world outside the small circle of pain that was himself. He began to notice that whatever he was riding was not moving as violently as it had been a moment before, was no longer trying to throw him back into the water. He opened his eyes to a dazzling world of brilliant colour. He shut them again, blinked and squinted through half-closed lids to try and make sense of where he was.

He saw tree bark, thick and deeply cracked, shining wet and slimy with green stuff. It was the trunk of an enormous tree. He was lying face down on it, and it was moving quite fast along the foaming surface of a river: it must be the same river he had glimpsed from the Dome of ArcOne.

The river banks were quite close to him. At times his log passed directly beneath the shadow of one or other of them. But there was no possibility of stopping his log and scrambling ashore. Apart from the speed at which the river was carrying him along, the banks themselves were of dark shiny rock, split into vertical fissures, with no horizontal layers or shelves that he might use for hand or foot hold. Above the steep banks he could glimpse huge trees sliding by, maddeningly out of reach.

Tomi raised his head cautiously and looked ahead. The river cut a channel through the black rock, sometimes turning to left or right, so that the current, and his log borne on it, swerved from right to left bank and back. Now and then a brilliance struck the water and turned it into molten metal. At first he couldn't imagine what it was, because when his log reached these stretches of water they seemed no different from the others.

A sudden comforting warmth on his soaked and freezing back made him look up into a brilliance a thousand times brighter than the most powerful light on ArcOne. The sun! As it had been in his dream . . . only this was real!

For a moment the realization that he was actually out of doors, under the naked sky and the raw and burning sun, so terrified him that he clung to his wet cold log with his eyes tightly shut. He trembled. What am I to do? What *can* I do?

Hang on. Look around. Observe. Keep calm. His lifepak spoke to him and the familiar voice in his head soothed his fears. Were all his paks intact, undamaged by his fall and the water? Yes, it seemed so. Their weight on his back made him feel strong again and able to face whatever lay ahead.

He opened his eyes and looked around again. The river was definitely slowing down. The trees above his head were not moving by so fast. The river was getting wider too, which wasn't such a good thing, since he was farther from shore than he had been before. But the banks seemed to be getting lower, so that if he could get out of the current he should be able to get ashore without too much difficulty.

All he had to do was to obey his lifepak, hang on, keep from panicking and wait until the current slackened enough to allow him to paddle his log boat to shore. Then he would walk upstream until he got back to ArcOne. The slave revolt would be safely over and he would earn a hero's welcome.

He began to feel quite pleased with himself, in spite of the icy coldness of his body and the various cuts and bruises that were beginning to make themselves felt. I must remember to thank Seventy-Three for saving my life, he thought. I could ask Father to give her a present... but what would be useful to a slave?

A sudden wave from the left buffeted his log and he almost slipped off. In sudden panic he clutched at it, his nails digging into the rotting bark. The buffeting did not last long. The river smoothed out again. It was curving way over to the right around a big bulge of low meadowland. Could he paddle out of the current to the right bank and get ashore?

He remembered his Dreamland experience and lay forward, stroking down into the water with his left hand, trying to push the nose of the log over to the right, out of the current. But the river held the log as firmly in its grip as a magnet holds iron filings. After he had paddled like this for a long time, until his shoulder ached and his hand was numb, he was still caught in the current.

A sudden riffle of white water nearly tipped him off again. He gave up trying to steer and concentrated on hanging on.

Time passed. The wide curve to the right stopped and he could see over to the left that the land fell away into a low green slope almost level with the river itself. The comforting sun disappeared behind the tree-covered hills to his right. Dark shadows lay across the river, turning the water from greyish green to a flat slate grey that grew darker even as he watched it. His body began to shiver in small spasmodic shakes that turned into deep uncontrollable shudders. His teeth chattered and he clenched them. He shut his eyes again and concentrated on hanging on, his whole being contracted into the small warm kernel in the middle of him.

THE LOG bucked violently and his eyes flew open. There was land close at hand on his left. Reeds bent under the log. Dead branches poked out of the water. Tomi drew up his cold cramped legs and got ready. The next time the log caught and hesitated against a dead branch he rolled off into the water.

He gasped, staggered and clutched at the dead wood. It broke off in his hand. He fell forward into the water and on hands and knees crawled across slippery stones and crushed reeds to the shore.

He lay there with his eyes shut, his face in a pool of slime, a branch sticking into his side. Safe! He was safe!

After a while he crawled another metre or two onto a dry grassy area. There he collapsed again.

HIS EYES opened to blackness. He sat up quickly, wondering where under the Dome he was, and yelled with pain. Every square centimetre of skin felt cut or bruised. Then he remembered and groaned. He was sick with cold and the front of his stomach felt as if it were glued to the back. How long since he had eaten?

He crawled painfully down to the water and washed the dried mud from his face and drank a little to fill the emptiness of his stomach. Not much. The water was so cold that it made his teeth ache. He began to shiver again.

A fire! If he were to survive until the sun came up he must have a fire. What had Denn said in the dream? "It's easy; all you have to do is to rub two sticks together." Something like that. It seemed an unlikely way of making fire. He accessed his historypak, but all he got was something called 'matches' and something else called a 'tinderbox'.

He shivered and felt around for dry wood. At least there was plenty of it here, wherever *here* was. Once he got a spark there would be no problem feeding it. He gathered a rough pile together and then found two straight sticks, by feel more than sight. Obviously he needed to generate enough heat through friction for combustion to take place. A drill would be the most efficient way. He accessed 'drill" in his pak and set to work.

He sharpened an end of one of his sticks against a stone until it had a decent point. Then he pushed the point into a natural dent in his second piece of wood. He held the second piece of wood steady against his foot while moving his hands as fast as he could to and fro against the drill piece. He did this for a long time. The only heat seemed to be generated in the palms of his hands, rather than in the wood. In the end he threw the sticks away, rolled himself into a tight ball with his arms hugging his chest, and tried to go to sleep.

After a while he turned over. Maybe he would be more comfortable on his right side. A stone dug painfully into his hip. He pried it out of the dirt with his fingernails and threw it away. He pulled up all the long grass he could reach and made it into a wad to support his neck. If only he weren't so cold and hungry he would be able to sleep.

In ArcOne everyone would be sleeping. Oh, if only he were back in his warm bed, with the computer to tell him when to sleep and when to wake. Why wasn't his lifepak helping him to go to sleep? His infopaks worked all right. Why couldn't he sleep? It was ridiculous to be awake in the middle of the night.

He groaned and struggled up on one elbow. Above his head the stars were a bright scatter of cold points of light. He stared until they slowly sorted themselves into patterns he could recognize. He accessed Astronomy. Yes, there was Andromeda... there Casseiopeia. And Ursa Minor low down in the north, up river, right over the place where ArcOne must be.

His astropak had never told him how very far away the stars would look, how very empty the spaces between them, how very lonely a single person on the surface of the planet Earth must feel, staring up at them, seeing them stare coldly down.

"I want to go home. Oh, I want to go home." But his voice made the loneliness more intense. There was no other human sound. Nothing but the liquid murmur of the river and the dry whisper of wind in the reeds. He crouched down in the grass and wept. After a long time he fell asleep.

HE WOKE, stiff and sore, hungrier than ever. He pushed himself onto his knees and used a sapling to haul himself to his feet. The ceremonial toga that had probably saved his life, wrapped around his body with air trapped within its folds, was now a damp creased mess. He stripped it off, shook it out and hung it over a bush to dry in the sun. Then he looked down to see what had happened to him.

Both knees were raw and there was a long but shallow gash on his right thigh. Purple bruises had come up across his belly and on his arms and legs. What had happened after the sleeping gas had hit him? He must have turned as he fell and landed face down in the sewer that had shot him with the City waste out into the river. That would account for the bruises and scrapes. If he'd landed on his back his paks would have been torn right off. He was lucky – up to a point.

Only what now? He clutched his drooping belly. He had no idea that hunger would hurt so much. In all his life the only pain he had suffered had been from over-eating. Oh, how he hurt! He had got to find something to eat.

Dressed in his underpants and shirt and sandals he picked his way along the shore, looking for a likely place to fish. It was easy, Denn had said. Find a pool where the fish lie still and just hook them through the gill flaps with your fingers. Nothing to it. But then in the dream Denn had said that making fire was easy too. Even if he did catch a fish, could he bear to eat it raw? He shuddered.

43

Slowly he made his way back along the shore to where he had hung his toga. There was a brisk breeze off the river and the sun was rising above the hill. His toga was dry enough to wear.

He put it on carefully, draping the folds precisely around his infopaks. He would not try to make a fire. He would not waste time trying to fish. He would set out immediately to walk back to ArcOne. It couldn't be far upriver. If he started right away he might be back in time for lunch. He should certainly be back for dinner. All he had to do was to follow the river upstream. There was no way he could get lost. It was a pity he was on the left bank instead of the right. But the river was too wide to think of crossing here. He would find ArcOne and then think about crossing the river.

He began to walk briskly along the shore. After a few minutes he found that sandals designed for the stroll from apartment to dining hall to library or study were not the best kind of footwear to protect toes and ankles from stones, sharp reeds and unexpected pieces of dead wood. He limped painfully on.

Before long he noticed a dazzle of light in his eyes. He was facing east instead of north. He must be on a deep bay, he told himself. In a minute or two the shore will straighten out and turn north again.

The sun began to warm his left cheek. Then his back. He stopped, looked around puzzled, and saw something on the ground that set his heart pounding. Footprints! He was not alone. There was someone else, perhaps someone as knowledgeable as Denn, who could make a fire and catch fish. "Hi!" he yelled. "Where are you?"

A waterbird flapped noisily out of the reeds and set his heart pounding. Then there was silence. He looked all round, and with a swoop of despair realized that he had been staring at his own footprints. He had walked in a complete circle. Yet he had never left the shoreline. He was not on the bank of the river leading north to ArcOne, but on an island.

He began to run, following his previous footsteps, stumbling over hidden roots and broken branches. When the sun was full on his face he stopped and looked at the water. It flowed past his feet from left to right, and there, maybe a couple of hundred metres away, was the true shore. He had no food. No fire. No way of getting to shore. His knees gave way and he dropped to the ground. Maybe it would have been better if Seventy-Three had left him to have his throat cut. It would have been a quicker death than starvation.

Beyond the island's rim the water moved smoothly, like a loom full of finest synthetic. A bird perched on a stone above the water and dunked its head, fluffed up its wings and flew off. For an instant he found he was smiling. The bird was so small, so impertinent, to use the great river for its bath.

Tomi began to get angry. I am fourteen years old, he told himself, or the empty river or the island. I am the New Lord of Bentt. I have accessed more knowledge than any of the other Young Lords. It's stupid to die now. I won't die. "I won't," he shouted.

He scrambled to his feet and looked at his island. It was perhaps a hundred metres long and half as wide, though the irregular shoreline had made it seem larger at first. It was not very high. The central hill, on which stood a clump of trees, was no more than ten metres above the river level. The land close to the shore, now a tangle of scrub, reeds and washed-up timber, was probably under water every spring.

There seemed to be nothing actually living on the island, though birds roosted in the central clump of trees. He crossed and then recrossed it a few metres further on, searching the scrub for something to eat or something that might be useful to him.

Two-thirds of the way along he found a bramble thicket laden with purple black berries. He reached out and one of them fell plumply into his palm at the touch. It was delicious, sweet and tangy, full of juice. He squatted by the thicket and methodically stripped off the berries until his stomach felt satisfied. Then he went on.

45

By the time he had reached the downstream point of the island he had found nothing else that seemed useful. Unless a person could eat grass or leaves? If the worst came to the worst he could try them. Now his stomach was full he could more cheerfully face the fact that he could not live on the island. That he must find a way of getting off or die of starvation.

Knowledge is power – his infopak reminded him.

"Yes, I know. Tell me what to do?" he asked, but there was no answer. Why should there be? He had to ask first. He sat on a fallen tree and methodically accessed all of his great store of information: ancient history, engineering, story, myth, mathematics, and he asked: "How do you cross a fast river when you are unable to swim and there is no bridge?"

His paks gave him many answers from Bridges, suspension, to Bridges, pontoon. From Outrigger, Canoe, Kayak, to Raft, inflatable, and Raft, balsawood. He lingered on the last suggestion and asked for more information.

Balsawood, his wordpak told him, was a tropical South American tree with a very light strong wood. Well, he was not likely to find any balsawood trees here. Light and strong... He idly broke a dry branch from the tree where he sat and tossed it into the water. It dipped under, bobbed up and was borne rapidly along on the current.

Suppose he were to gather all the long straight pieces of wood he could find and tie them together in a kind of mat... Tie them with what? Access again: Rope, grass. Rope, hemp. Rope, synthetic. Synthetic. If he could tear his toga into strips they would certainly be strong enough. He was strangely reluctant to destroy his mother's gift, but he tugged at the loose end. It was far too tightly woven. With a knife or scissors, perhaps... but he had neither.

Rope, grass... Well, the island was certainly well supplied with grass. In fact, now he looked more closely he could see that there was the fine stuff that grew inland under the trees, coarse grass among the brush and brambles, and sedges and reeds that stood by the shore with their roots in the water. They were by far the longest and should make his job easier.

He girded his toga around his waist and waded into the shallows. The sedges were certainly strong. When he grasped a handful and pulled, the edges cut the palm of his hands. In the end he learned to protect his palms with wads of soft inland grass. Before long he had a whole pile of sedge.

He sat down to plait and knot the lengths into the semblance of a rope. Hope began to rise within him. He worked hard and was startled to notice that the sun had moved to the centre of the river and it was noon.

He coiled the lengths of rope he had made and started to search for straight pieces of wood. He found most of them on the upstream end of the island, where there was almost a dump of stuff that had come downriver and been caught by the tangle of wood already there. By evening he had laid out a mat of wood pieces about two metres long and a metre wide. Then it was too dark to see any more.

In the remaining wisps of twilight he pulled up as much soft grass as he could and piled it in a dry depression beneath the trees at the centre of the island, out of the wind. Then he drank as much water as he could stomach, wishing it were solid food. He burrowed into his newly made bed.

In his whole life he had never worked as hard as he had done this day, and he fell asleep without even thinking about it. Later he was awakened by a sound. Had it been a sound? He lay tensely listening. There it was! Hoo... hoo. A cold and sorrowful sound from a tree close above his head. He could feel the gooseflesh creep up his arms. He crouched in his grass bed until a pale clumsy shape suddenly dropped from the tree and flapped off across the dark water.

Later in the night he woke from a dream in which he was gobbling huge mounds of soyburgers, slabs of soy cheese, dozens of boiled eggs, hectares of vegetables, until his stomach hurt. When he woke his stomach was still hurting. He folded his hands across its emptiness and at length went back to sleep.

He woke again to a grey pre-dawn world. All the colours seemed to have been drained out of the landscape and everything looked flat and unreal. A faint mist smoked off the river. It was very quiet. Even the voice of the river was hushed.

He got up and went to look at his raft. It wasn't bad. He squatted beside it and began to interlace the pieces of wood with the lengths of grass rope. He worked without looking up until he had a flexible mat. Would that work? Shouldn't the raft be rigid?

He could tie two or three thick branches at right angles to the others. And he would need something better than his hand to force the raft across the current to the bank. He set off to look for suitable wood.

By now the sun was up and the mist was off the water. He passed the bramble thicket and stopped to search for more berries. There was hardly a berry left. He popped the few he could find into his mouth and wished he had not been so greedy the day before.

A spoonful of berries wasn't much of a breakfast for a Lord. How long until his next meal? he thought, as he hauled the wood he had found down to the shore. Then he found he had to make more rope to fasten the cross members to his raft. By the time he was finished the sun was again touching the western hills.

"I won't spend another night in this place," he told himself. He had got into the habit of talking out loud as he worked. It made him feel a little less alone.

He tied his last piece of rope firmly to the raft and fastened the other end to a bush close to shore. Then he heaved the raft onto its side. It was quite a weight. He gave it a push and it flopped smack into the water. And it floated! The river caught at it, tugging eagerly. The raft bobbed, held only by its tether of rope.

Tomi swallowed. The water seemed so smooth and calm on top and yet beneath the surface was hidden this wild power. Dare he trust himself to this homemade contraption of wood and sedge?

"It's that or starve to death," he told himself. "Get it over with, while it's still light. Come on."

48

He girded his toga tightly around his middle, just in case. Paddle in hand he stepped aboard the raft and fell hastily to his knees as it rocked wildly and threatened to spill him into the water. With his added weight the raft was now awash, but at least it wasn't sinking. He reached back to untie the rope from the bush and then quickly dug his rough paddle into the water, aiming at a spot he had marked out on the river bank opposite, where a clump of white-barked trees grew.

He found to his despair that though he could keep the front of the raft pointing towards the trees it was still being swept firmly downstream. He paddled harder and harder until his arms were trembling and the sweat was pouring down his body. But it was hopeless. The best he could do was to hold a position in the middle of the stream. His heart was thudding and his head felt as if it were being squeezed by two giant hands.

He gasped and stopped paddling. At once the current took the raft as if it were a leaf. He pulled himself back to his knees and tried to concentrate on steering the raft slowly towards the bank. In the end he got the knack of it, but for each twenty metres or so downstream, he gained only a metre towards the shore.

His island was out of sight by the time he finally left the grip of the current and reached the shallows. He looked quickly about, saw a broad shallow beach, where the river bank had been undercut and broken down, and paddled straight for it.

The last rays of the sun were touching the hill above him when he abandoned his raft and crawled thankfully onto dry land. He fell into the sweet grass and lay there with his face buried, listening to the rasping of his breath and the thud of blood in his ears. He rolled over onto his back as far as his bulky paks would allow. The grass crushed beneath his weight, smelling of the sun. He took a deep thankful breath and closed his eyes.

HE WOKE, freezing cold, to the now familiar stars. He stood up to unhitch his toga from around his middle and wrap it around him like a blanket. How strange the river looked, quite unearthly, as if he had been transported in his sleep to another world. It shone with a cold radiance. On the river bank opposite, each tree stood out dark and straight. It was beautiful and absolutely terrifying. Where was the unearthly white light coming from that made it all as bright as day and yet changed everything into something else?

He turned his head to the left and cried out in shock. Over the hills above the left riverbank was an enormous white circle, as hard-edged as if cut out of beryllium. It hung above him, close enough to touch, only he would never dare. It seemed to be staring down at him, challenging his right to be there. He felt the skin on his neck and naked head creep and tighten with fear.

Then the shining disc met a wisp of cloud and slid behind it. Tomi's sense of perspective was restored. He was looking at the moon. The moon! He accessed it in his astropak.

Moon: Earth's satellite. Diameter 3,476 kilometres. Mean distance from Earth 384 thousand kilometres. Orbital period 27.3 days. Mass... he cut off the unwanted information. It had nothing to say to this incredible beauty.

He accessed literature and into his mind came the words:

'Slowly, silently, now the moon
Walks the night in her silver shoon.'

Other quotations crowded eagerly in, but Tomi liked the first one best. It felt good and he repeated it in a whisper to the still night. His fear had gone, but he shivered and was suddenly aware that he was standing in his underclothing with only a layer of fine synthetic between his skin and the chilly breeze. He should look for a more sheltered place to spend the rest of the night.

He moved up the slope away from the river, his way lit by the brilliant moon. Walking seemed simple at first, but after he had tripped over a fallen tree that he had thought was a shadow, and edged carefully across a smooth carpet of grass striped with seemingly solid shadows, he gave up. There was a little hollow that seemed to hold some of the day's warmth. It would have to do. He curled up and pulled the long grass down over him.

THE NEXT MORNING was also grey, with mist lying over everything like a tatter of grey fabric and drops of water on every seedhead and blade of grass. Before he had walked more than a few metres his legs and the bottom of his already damp toga were soaked. Then it began to rain, softly. He soon found that he could not follow the shore itself. The bank was littered with dead wood and in places had broken away and fallen into the river. Further inland the ground sloped gently up to his right, eventually steepening into a tree-covered mountain. The lower grassy slopes made for comfortable walking. He set out in a grey drizzle.

By noon the sky had cleared and the sun was sucking moisture up out of the ground. He reached the slope above his island. How tiny and barren it looked from up here. It gave him a pang of dismay to realise what a long way he must still have to go. At this rate it would take days to reach ArcOne. He would get weaker and weaker and die of starvation... He sat down on the warm damp grass to rest and think about it.

In the last stretch of his nightmare journey downstream on the log, he seemed to remember that the river had made a wide curve westward and then a swoop back to the east. Surely that must be the bump in the landscape just ahead of him? If he were to cut due north over this hill he would save hours of time. He couldn't possibly get lost because the river would still be there on his left beyond the hill.

He took off his sandals. His feet smarted painfully and on both heels the skin was red and puffed up in watery blisters. He cooled them in the damp grass and couldn't bear the thought of putting his sandals on again. He knotted them around his neck and struggled to his feet with a groan.

51

Before long he was completely out of sight of the river. Dead ahead, beyond the gentle rise of green, he could see a broad escarpment between two high mountains. It lay roughly north, and on this feature he kept his eyes.

He walked doggedly on. The sun was on his left now, sinking rapidly towards the hills that lay beyond the river. Before long he would have to stop and find a place to sleep again. He ran his tongue over his cracked lips and stood still in dismay. Fool! He had no water, not a single drop. Over to his left litres and litres of it poured down. It was too cruel. The hunger pains were bad enough, but how long would he have to endure thirst before he came on the river again?

"I'll go on walking," he said grimly. "Once the moon is up I'll be able to see. I'll walk until I'm over the hill and down in the valley again. Then I'll drink and drink..." He ran his thick tongue over his cracked lips and plodded on.

He had to rest for a while, but when the moon rose he went on. He could no longer see the escarpment between the two mountains that had been his guide to the north, but he kept as straight a course as he could, and Ursa Minor, low in the north, kept him on track.

He walked on, no longer feeling the pain in his feet or his empty belly, nor the stiffness in his legs or back. The moon cast a silver trail up the hillside and Tomi followed it as if he were sleepwalking.

Suddenly, with a heart-stopping thud, he fell forward onto his fat stomach with a crash that knocked the wind out of him. He tried to pull his knees up to his chest, wheezing, struggling to catch his breath, but something was holding his left foot. He fell on his side and gagged and retched. His empty stomach hurt abominably. He groaned and clutched at the grass.

When he had recovered he sat up and struggled to free his foot. He found a snare of finely plaited grass so tightly caught around his ankle that the flesh had puffed up and it took both hands to ease the noose off his foot. He could see that it had been a trap. There were the two twigs that held the noose

52

upright. There was the forked stick that held the other end securely to the ground.

A snare meant edible meat. He thought of replacing it and lurking close by in case something ran into it as he had. But the problems of a fire to cook with and a knife to skin and dismember his catch made it all quite impractical. Anyway he had probably frightened away anything within kilometres with the noise he had made.

He got painfully to his feet. The last handful of berries seemed to have been digested weeks and weeks ago. He was getting thin. His underwear hung loosely on him and he had to bind his toga tightly around his waist to stop his undershorts from slipping off.

He had trudged another fifty metres along the moon's path when a sudden thought stopped him in midstride. He stumbled. Fool! Idiot! A snare meant the presence of human beings to set it. He wasn't alone in this vast wilderness after all. Somewhere, within a day's walk, maybe closer, were other human beings.

He called out, suddenly desperate for company. His voice dropped among the trees and the grass without even an echo. He called again and strained his ears, but only silence answered. He was too far away to hear even the voice of the river.

Lonelier than ever before he limped on until the moon set and he could go no further. He didn't bother looking for a comfortable place, but wrapped his toga around him and collapsed where he had stopped.

HE HAD NOT been walking for long the next morning before he found that he was once more going downhill towards the river. He limped on. His eyes were hot and the lids gummed up. His face felt stiff and his mouth was like sand. The slope steepened and fell away beneath his feet so that he had to hang on to the trees that now grew more closely together. He came upon the river so suddenly that he almost fell into it.

53

High above it was a tree whose roots hung half exposed over a place where the soil had fallen away from the bank. He could climb down beside it. But would he be able to get up again?

The water spoke softly of coolness, wetness; stomach filling, soothing to sunburnt face and head. Tomi stripped off his toga and knotted one end to the tree just above its roots. The other end hung free a couple of metres above the shore.

"If I get trapped down there I'll die... but if I don't get something to drink, I'll certainly die."

He slipped over the bank feet first and scrambled down with the help of his toga rope. He let go and landed on a narrow strip of earth that gave, but then held firm. He fell on his stomach and scooped cold water into his mouth and over his head and face. He went on splashing in a kind of ecstasy long after the real need was gone.

At last he got to his feet and reached up for the end of the toga. It dangled just beyond the tips of his outstretched fingers. He gave a feeble spring upwards. Not quite enough. He gathered together strengths he did not know he possessed, jumped wildly, caught the end of the toga and clawed his way upward, his bare feet pushing at the falling dirt and stones and tangled roots.

After he had rested he untied the toga from the tree and knotted it carelessly around his middle before climbing up the hill to a place level enough for walking. It was not easy to find. The smooth meadowland was gone. Now the trees crowded closely together, with thicket between them instead of grass. At last he found a narrow beaten path which he guessed must have been made by small animals. It wandered up and down, skirting the thickest masses of brush, but it headed more or less in the direction he wanted to go – upriver.

He trudged along, stopping only when he came upon a creeper bearing smooth berries of dark red. Remembering the delightful meal on the island he didn't hesitate to start picking them and stuffing them in his mouth. They had a bitter aftertaste, with none of the sweet juiciness of the others, but he told himself that at least they would fill him. After a few mouthfuls he felt sick and stopped eating. "It's because I've been so long without food," he told himself. He walked on slowly. In spite of all the water he had drunk his mouth felt very dry. He looked over to the left to see if the river were close enough for another drink. The trees seemed to double, turn misty and dance in front of his eyes. A sudden shaft of sunlight cut through the trees and stabbed into his head like a knife. He clutched at a tree. "Tired, that's all. Have a bit of a rest. Go on later." He fell clumsily to his knees, his face in the dead leaves, his fat bottom sticking up in the air. He wasn't comfortable, but he felt too tired and sick to move.

After he had been motionless for some time a squirrel, which had been busy all day collecting nuts for its winter store, decided it would be safe to take a short cut by his body. It stopped right in front of him, wrinkling up its nose and twinkling its silky whiskers. Tomi did not move.

4
Rowan

Tomi was inside a soft plastic cocoon that shut out cold and hunger and pain. He would do very well if only they would leave him alone. "Go away!" His voice was thick and far away, like a stranger's.

"Ah-ha! So the skinhead can talk, can he?" A woman's voice, or a girl's.

Slowly Tomi became aware that the cocoon was himself, and that the Other was furiously rubbing his arms and legs. His eyes flickered open to unbearably bright light and he closed them with a cry of pain. He felt an arm under his shoulders and something hard and cool against his mouth.

"Drink," the voice ordered.

He drank obediently. It was horribly bitter, and the cupful had hardly landed in his stomach when it came up again. He rolled over onto his side, groaning and retching.

"Good," the distant voice approved. He would have argued, but he hadn't the strength. His face was wiped with a cool wet cloth and he was ordered to drink again. He shook his head and wished that he hadn't, as it went on spinning long after he had stopped shaking it. His whole body was whirling round in a funnel that led down to nothingness.

He groaned and leaned back against the Other's shoulder. The cup was pushed against his lips and some of its contents trickled down his throat. It was water this time, clean and sweet. With a feeble hand he helped tip the cup to his mouth.

Then there was a dream of movement. Of lying still, but with the sound of grass swishing beneath him and the smell of crushed herbs close to his face. Plants softly brushed his sides. He slept.

He woke ravenously hungry. Whatever had been wrong with his eyes had righted itself. Things were in focus and the light no longer hurt. He found that he was lying on his back looking up at a ceiling which seemed to have been made out of thin tree trunks laid closely together, rather like his raft. The surface he was on was hard, but padded with furry cloth. As he moved pain shot from his shoulders into his head. His paks had dug into him as he slept and now the pain was excruciating. He eased himself onto one elbow with a groan and looked around.

He was in a small square room whose walls were made of horizontally laid tree trunks. The only light came, not from overhead, but from a small window to his left and an open door beyond the foot of the bed.

The golden squares of light were inviting, and he swung his legs off the bed and stood up unsteadily. Why, he was as weak as an infant! What had happened to him and where in the Dome was he? He staggered over to the door and grabbed the frame, stepped through it into a sunny glade surrounded by wooden houses. There was a fire burning in the centre, and the mouthwatering smell of food drifted towards him.

Stiff-legged, Tomi crossed the glade and stared down at the fire. There were clay pots propped on stones and a lump of strange stuff that hung above the flames, hissing drops of fatty liquid into the fire beneath. The smell was overwhelming. He reached out a hand.

"What do you think you're doing?" He spun round at the accusing voice. A young girl, hands on her hips, was glaring at him in a most unwomanly way. Her head wasn't clean, but covered with long red hair, and she wore a tunic of the same furry stuff that had covered his bed.

"Get me some food. I'm hungry," he ordered.

57

She laughed and Tomi flushed angrily. No one, not even one's best friend, laughed at a Lord. "Get me some food at once!"

She strolled across the grass towards him. Her feet were bare, the nails rough and broken, and her legs were a golden brown except for the white scars of thorn scratches.

"Supper is not ready yet. We do not eat until the others come home from hunting."

"But I'm starved. I've eaten nothing for days!"

She laughed again and covered her mouth with a small brown hand. Above her hand her eyes danced. "You could last all winter on that belly. Why, you're as fat as a bear."

"Don't you dare to speak to me like that. I'll have you know I am the New Lord Tomi of Bentt."

The irritating girl sketched a mock curtsey, her mouth turned down solemnly at the corners, though her eyes still danced. They were strange eyes, half green, half flecked with brown. Not exactly beautiful, but interesting. He was determined that she should take him seriously.

"Listen to me." He stamped his foot. It landed on a pebble and he yelped with pain. He had forgotten that his feet were bare. He felt so angry he would have hit her, but perhaps it would be more useful to make friends. She belonged in this savage world Outside. Without her help he might starve. Without her help he would not find the way home to ArcOne.

He stood, rubbing his sore foot, wondering what to talk about. He quickly accessed his infopaks on subjects of conversation with savages, but could find nothing in the least useful. As he stood with his mouth open, she turned her back and began to walk away.

"Oh, look, don't go. I'm..." He stopped. She had only gone into one of the wooden huts and now came back with a small bowl in her hand. She stooped over the fire and scooped liquid from one of the simmering pots.

"There. You may have this broth to last you until suppertime. Don't drink it too fast or you will be ill again. Drink." She held out the bowl.

58

Tomi drew back. "I've heard your voice before. It was you... you gave me poison. You made me sick."

"I saved your life, skinhead. If I had not forced you to wake up and drink my herbs you would be dead of poison berries."

"They were poisonous? I... I did not know. I ate berries the day before and they were very good."

She rolled her eyes upward. "Aha! So all roots and berries in the world are good to eat, are they? What a clever young man you are. Why, not one of our smallest children would have eaten berries from the red-fruit vine."

He flushed. "Well, how should I know? I'm not a savage."

She drew back frowning. Then she smiled. "No, that is right. I remember. You are the New Lord Bentt. And what are you doing here eating poison berries and talking to savages, Lord Tomi of Bentt?"

He hesitated, conscious of offending her, and not sure how to put it right. Not sure if he *wanted* to put it right. She squatted by the fire and motioned him to sit beside her.

"Come, drink." She held out the cup and he took it from her and sipped it cautiously. It was very hot. As he swallowed, new strength flooded through his body. He drained the cup and held it out for more, but she shook her head and took the cup from him. "So what are you doing here, Tomi of Bentt?" she asked again.

He sat beside her and told her the story of the slave revolt and his brush with death at the hands of the rebels and in the river. The dimples faded from her cheeks as he talked. She held out her hands to the fire as if she were suddenly cold.

"...so I followed the river north again," he concluded. "By now I must be very close to ArcOne. If you can just show me the way."

She shook her head slowly, her hair falling forward so he could not see her face.

"But it can't be far. It *can't*. I've walked upstream for two days."

"There is no place such as you describe on this river," she said slowly, as if choosing her words.

59

"Perhaps you haven't travelled far enough north. If you were to go another day's walk upriver?"

"We know our river to its source. There *is* no such place."

Tomi's head sank to his knees. "It can't have vanished. The City is real. I've lived there all my life. This is the dream. And I'm trapped in it. What is to become of me?"

She touched his shoulder. "You are welcome to make your home with us. My name is Rowan." She told it as if the telling were a gift.

He looked blankly around the sunlit clearing, at the semi-circle of rough wooden huts, at the stone-ringed fireplace with its array of crude pots, at the long-haired girl in her shaggy tunic. He drew the filthy remnants of his toga around him. "I want to go home." His head sank to his knees.

After he had raised his head and scrubbed the wetness off his cheeks he found that he was alone. How dared she leave without asking permission, he thought angrily. Then he remembered the light touch of her hand on his shoulder and the tone of her voice: "You are welcome."

Welcome. Nobody had ever said that to him before. But of course there had been no need. As son of the Lord Bentt his welcome had been taken for granted. Then he had earned through his skill and hard work the right to be called Young Lord. And then New Lord. It had all been his, until the ungrateful wicked slaves had snatched it from him. "It's not fair." He wept again. "I want to go home."

He was huddled over the fire when voices among the trees made him stir and then jump to his feet, alarmed. Then he saw it was Rowan. But she was no longer alone. With her was a boy of about twelve and an older couple. All wore the same rough tunics and long hair. The man even had a brown curly beard that swept his chest. Savages, thought Tomi in disgust. I have fallen among savages.

He heard Rowan's voice, high and excited. "I couldn't have left him to die, could I? What harm can he do? He's only a boy, a dull fat boy."

He watched them cross the clearing with resentment boiling inside him. Dull? Fat? He'd show them. He flung his toga over his shoulder.

"Tomi, this is my mother. Her name is Healhand. My father, who is called Swift. And this is my little brother, Arbor."

"Little indeed! You just wait, sister. In another year I'll pick you up in one hand as I saw Groundsel do the other day."

Rowan didn't answer, but Tomi saw her blush a warm rose under the golden brown of her skin.

Swift held out his hand. After a second's hesitation, Tomi took it. The clasp was firm and he could feel the man's strength in the toughness of his calloused palm. "You are welcome."

He used the same words as Rowan. Perhaps it was a formal greeting among these people, similar to the Lord's: 'May your paks grow heavier.'

But Swift's eyes did not match his cordial words. They narrowed and looked Tomi up and down suspiciously. "And what might you be doing so far...?" he began.

"I've told Tomi over and over again that there is no underground city on the banks of our river," Rowan interrupted rudely, in a way no City girl would ever be allowed to. "But that's where he says he's from. An underground city called ArcOne. He didn't believe me. No, you didn't, Tomi. I could tell by your face."

"But it doesn't make sense. ArcOne is built right on the west side of the river, high above the rapids. When I finally got ashore I travelled north up the east bank. The City *must* be ahead. How could you miss it? A Dome a kilometre across and a dam on the river..."

"But it's not..." Arbor began, and Tomi saw Rowan kick his ankle with a hard brown foot. Perhaps in this society sons were not as important as daughters, and that was what made her so unbearably bossy.

"I assure you there is no such place on this river," Swift said.

61

"Then what am I to *do*?"

"Stay with us," said Rowan. Healhand and Swift exchanged glances. "It's the only way," Rowan pleaded.

"But I don't *want* to stay. I want to go home. I know! I must go downstream again to my island and somehow cross to the western bank. I wish I had tied up my raft."

Swift and Healhand exchanged another of those puzzling looks. "Stay for a while," Healhand said gently. "You are tired and badly sunburnt. The sun is still hot on a naked head at noon. In a few weeks it will be cooler and your hair will have grown."

"My hair..." Tomi put a hand to his scalp. An unpleasant stubble gritted against his fingers. "Yuch! I shall look like a slave."

Rowan opened her mouth and closed it again. Arbor flushed angrily.

"Stay then," Healhand urged.

"You *have* to," Rowan put in.

"Not if he doesn't want to," Swift's voice was firm. "We are all free, Rowan, remember. You are free to stay with us, Tomi, to share our shelter and food and learn to gather food yourself, to repair and clean..."

"That is not Lord's work." Tomi drew himself up.

"Or you are free to leave." Swift went on as if Tomi hadn't spoken. "Free to move north or south, east or west. Free to be warm if you can make a fire, or to be cold if you cannot. Free to eat if you have the skill to snare an animal or go hungry if you cannot. Free to pick berries and dig roots, eat them and live – or die. Out here in the forest you are quite free."

Some choice, thought Tomi. He swallowed. "I will stay and learn your wilderness ways," he said in as lordly a manner as he could manage. "Then, once I have learned them, I will go in search of ArcOne again. But I do not cook or clean. That is slave's work. Or women's."

Arbor began to whistle between his teeth, a catchy tune. Rowan kicked him again. He grinned and dodged. Rowan was half laughing, half angry.

"Tomi, we share our labours here for the good of all," Healhand said kindly. "All of us take turns to do what has to be done. If you wish to have a bed and a meal you will help in the making of them."

"Would you let me starve?" His pudgy lip stuck out.

"I would not stop you if you chose to starve yourself, though I should be very unhappy. But it would be *your* choice, not mine."

"Well..." The smell of whatever it was roasting above the fire twisted his empty stomach. He swallowed a sudden gush of saliva. "What about tonight's meal? I didn't help make that."

She smiled. "That is our gift to you, if you choose to stay."

"Oh. Very well, I will stay." Tomi nodded graciously. I am far more intelligent than they are, he thought to himself. I will learn very fast how to hunt and to make fire. Then I will leave and find ArcOne. It *has* to be upriver. For some reason they are lying to me.

Suddenly there was the sound of voices and laughter, and the glade was crowded with people. Perhaps fifty, thought Tomi, each as savage as the next. They drew back when they first saw him, and one man actually raised a rough stone axe. But Swift and Healhand spoke quickly to them, and afterwards most of them behaved as if he were not there. Though now and again, unexpectedly, he would see a person look at him with an expression that was so strange he shivered.

Coarse wooden platters were brought out, and Swift used an ancient knife, its blade worn to a thin crescent by countless sharpenings, to cut up the food. There seemed to be no other utensils.

When I am ready to leave I will take that, thought Tomi. It will be very useful to have a knife.

Rowan handed him a platter and then sat down beside him and began to eat. He stared in dismay at the food. A great slab of stuff, fire-blackened at the edges and oozing red in the middle, a roasted root and a pile of what looked like weeds. And how was he supposed to eat with neither knife nor fork?

63

He watched Rowan tear a fibrous strip and stuff it in her mouth. Red juice ran down her chin and she scooped it back in with one brown finger. Cautiously he tore off a small piece and put it in his mouth. It took a lot more chewing than soyburgers, but he had to admit it was full of flavour. He felt warm inside and suddenly courageous. He swallowed, tore off another strip and pushed it into his mouth. The juice squirted out onto the pale blue of his New Lord's toga. He blushed. What would his lady mother think to see him eat like this?

"What is this?" he asked as soon as his mouth was empty enough.

"Deer." Rowan tore off another piece.

"You mean – an animal?"

"Of course." She stared.

He swallowed. Of course. He knew about eating meat. He had been prepared for the idea when he had found the snare. He broke open his baked root and ate the mealy insides. Unlike the root in his Dreamland adventure it was filling, but very dull. The leaves and herbs tasted bitter and he pushed them off his plate into the grass, hoping Rowan wouldn't notice.

She cut herself another piece of meat and would have offered one to Tomi, but Healhand noticed and stopped her. "You will make Tomi ill. He mustn't eat too much at once."

He blushed angrily, remembering how Rowan had laughed at his fat. Healhand touched his arm. "I only meant that you have been without food for several days. You mustn't overstrain your stomach."

He felt better, though he pretended not to hear her, not to care. Instead he turned to look at the others gathered around the fire. There were about fifty of them, from old men and women to a few, a very few, small children. All of them were brown and had a carefree look, despite their thinness. The oddest thing about them was that they were all straightbacked, not bowed with learning like the Lords, nor with downcast eyes like slaves or workers. In a way they looked more like soldiers, though with no third eye strapped to their forehead, but they looked straight into each other's faces in a way that soldiers never would. Tomi had the strange feeling that they were proud of their straight backs and straight looks, as if they were saying: 'I am me. I am free.'

Ignorant savages! The phrase jumped into Tomi's mind and he felt better. After all, his back was bowed with knowledge, his head was shaven and his flesh was fat. That was how it should be. That was what it was to be a Lord. And the Lords were Power.

Only it was uncomfortable sitting among such strangers with no conversation and only the occasional furtive glance. He was quite glad when Healhand came back and suggested that he might like to go to bed. The small wooden huts all looked alike to him, but Healhand led him straight to the one he had occupied before. "It is empty just now. We always have at least one extra for..." She stooped to flick dust off the bed-covering, "for anyone who might chance by."

"Where is the bathroom?" he interrupted, not really listening.

"You mean showers or toilets? The river is our shower. You may wash tomorrow. The privy you will find fifty paces back among the trees. While you are gone I will find something to help your sunburn."

She left him to discover the privy for himself. When he came back, his nose wrinkled in distaste, he found on the wooden chest at the bottom of his bed a small stone dish covered with a leaf. In it were some herbs chopped up in grease. He rubbed the stuff over his face and arms and the top of his head, which was indeed painfully tender.

He climbed into bed and pulled the bedcoverings around him, trying to get comfortable. No matter how he lay the infopaks dug into his neck, and now he had thought about it, his sunburnt head and arms began to smart painfully. Finally he slept.

He was wakened by the sudden crack of a burning stick. A long way off he heard a vague growling animal sound and lay tense, remembering the wild beast of his Dreamland adventure.

It was still not quite dark, so he had not been asleep for long. In the silence he became aware of voices talking softly outside.

"...not Rowan's fault."

"I agree she couldn't possibly leave him to die."

"Why not?" A small crack of laughter.

"That is unworthy, Treefeller."

"I know." The sound of a sigh. "But..."

"...will we do?"

"Keep him here. Can't risk having him go..."

"I agree."

"I too. But..." The fire crackled and spat again and Tomi could hear no more. When it died down they – whoever they were – had either stopped talking or moved out of earshot.

He tried to make sense of the conversation. Obviously they had been talking about *him*. Rowan's fault for rescuing *him*? If that is what it had meant, they had been talking as if he were an enemy. But if he were, they should be glad to see the last of him. Yet they were anxious he should stay. It didn't make sense. He lay awake worrying about it, until at last he decided on a plan to call their bluff. Only then did he sleep, restlessly.

Once he heard people moving about he got up, wrapped his filthy toga around him and went out to use the disgusting privy. He found water in a clay bowl near the newly-made fire and used some of it to wash his face and hands. Rowan appeared as he was trying to dry on the corner of his toga. "This morning we go down to the river to swim. You look as if you could do with it. You look terrible."

"Not surprising after last night. How can you bear sleeping on a bed like a board?"

"Perhaps we find them all right because we don't have those... those stupid lumps on our necks."

Tomi flushed and drew himself up. "I have accessed more information than any New Lord in the history of the City," he boasted.

"Much good it's done you, hasn't it? You'd have died of starvation or poison without us."

While Tomi was furiously trying to think of something cutting to say, Healhand bustled over to them. "Rowan, you have work to do. Tomi, I have got a fresh tunic for you to wear when you have bathed. That robe is fit for nothing but cleaning cloths."

He clutched it. "It's mine. My mother had it woven especially for me."

"We share what we have. But very well. I will still give you a new tunic, made from animals killed by Swift, skinned by me and sewn by Rowan. You shall wash your own robe and mend it yourself if you have a mind to."

"I'm no woman!" he shouted. Several people turned round, their faces shocked and curious. "It's woman's work," he muttered.

"It's your robe." She turned to the fire and began to ladle liquid into bowls.

Tomi waited for someone to serve him breakfast, but no one did. In the end he went over to the fire and helped himself. There was a hot brew and bread, flat and hardcrusted. It hurt his teeth and he almost gave up until hunger gave him the idea of dipping it in his drink. As he sucked the bitter brew and mouthed the coarse bread he had a sudden picture of Seventy-Three standing at the serving table.

"Eggs today, Young Lord." He could almost hear her voice. Oh, it wasn't fair. How stupid of Seventy-Three to find him such a dangerous hiding place. She must have known he would slip. Maybe she had done it on purpose. He'd have her whipped when he got home. That would teach her...

"Come on. We're going down to the river." Rowan ran up.

Now was the moment to find out where he stood. "No, thank you." He got stiffly to his feet. All this savage squatting without couches was making his back ache. "It's time I set out for ArcOne."

"But you don't know... who told you...?" Rowan spluttered, turned bright red and looked round for help.

"Unless you know exactly where your home is you would be mad to leave. You would not last a day in the forest. It is a different world from the grassland below." Swift broke in, all reasonableness.

"I survived before."

"Not much you didn't," Rowan said bluntly.

"Now I know which berries are poisonous I shall be in no danger."

"Come, Tomi, don't be foolish." Swift came close. There were other men, whose names he did not yet know, standing casually close. He looked at their muscled arms and hard hands, their sinewed legs and straight backs. He shrugged. "Very well, I'll stay."

He had no intention of leaving yet anyway, but now he knew what he had suspected. He really was a prisoner, and they would not let him leave.

He smiled grimly to himself as he scrambled down the steep bank to the river. Two spits of gravel pointed crooked fingers into the water, making a sheltered bay. He saw the men and boys cross the upstream spit to wash on the further side. Tomi followed them with relief. For a horrible moment he thought these savages might even bathe together, men and women.

Once across the spit everyone stripped off tunic and breeches or loincloth and leapt into the water, laughing and splashing, picking up handfuls of sand to scrub their skins. Tomi slowly unwound his toga and dropped it onto a rock. Reluctantly he untied his sandals and slipped off his undershirt and shorts. The water looked cold and uninviting. He stood at the edge, his white belly puckered with gooseflesh, and put one toe into the water.

68

"Oh come on!" Arbor grabbed his hand and pulled him forward. He staggered off balance, shouted at the iciness of the water and fell face down.

He came up, spluttering, to see Arbor's laughing face in front of him. He scrambled to his feet, his fist doubled, and swung out. Arbor ducked, and Tomi's wrist was caught and held in a grip of flexsteel. He looked into the cold grey eyes of Groundsel's father – what was his name? – Treefeller.

"He pushed me under. Let me go."

"It was only play, boys' play."

"He had no right to touch me. I am a Lord."

"Here you are nothing until you have earned the right to a name of your own. Go wash yourself and clean your robe."

Furiously Tomi turned his back and stalked out of the river, blue and goosebumped all over. Someone had flung his dirty toga into the shallow water. He hadn't even a towel. Wet and shivering, he climbed into his light synthefab shorts and shirt.

Arbor sidled up to him. Tomi watched him cautiously. What would the young savage do now, knowing that Treefeller would protect him?

Arbor grinned. "Sorry you slipped. I really didn't mean it. Come on, I'll help you wash your robe."

"I don't need..." Tomi swallowed his angry words. He suddenly realized that if he made enemies of everyone then he would never learn all he needed to know to survive in the wilderness and escape back to ArcOne.

"Thank you," he managed to say stiffly, and followed Arbor to a flat place where the water ran over a smooth slab of stone.

"Swish it in the water like this." Arbor swished so vigorously that Tomi was splashed. "Then rub the dirty spots against the stone and swish some more."

"Where is the syndet?"

"What is syndet?" Arbor stared.

"Stuff to put in the water. It foams up and makes things clean."

69

"We just use water and stones. For cleaning pots there's a patch of fine white sand down river." Arbor pointed "Every few days we bring the pots and dishes down and give them a good scrub."

"I just don't believe this," Tomi muttered as he rubbed his mother's finest synthefab over the stones. Beneath the water the silver and green and purple of the border shone as brightly as jewels. The crest of the House of Bentt.

I'll never forget who I am or where I came from, no matter how long these savages make me stay or what they make me do, he promised himself.

After bathing, everyone straggled up the steep path to the glade. There was something in the air, a sense of excitement, of anticipation.

"What's going to happen?" Tomi asked Arbor.

"Sharing, of course. Whenever someone..." Rowan ran by, grabbed Arbor by the wrist and dragged him away. "Come on, lazy. No talk now. It's wood gathering time!"

But Tomi noticed that they didn't go to join the others, who were gathering an enormous pile of wood near the centre of the clearing. Instead Rowan pulled Arbor to one side and talked to him rapidly, frowning as if she were scolding. When she was through, Arbor ran to join the others with a look at Tomi over his shoulder that was half mischievous, half scared, as if there were a secret – a secret Tomi didn't share.

There were preparations for a feast, with roast meat in large quantities, and platters of vegetables and roots brought from a hut that Tomi guessed must be the store house. Curiously he wandered over and peered in. It was crammed with food. There were mounds of roots on platforms raised off the dirt floor, big bowls of dried berries, flat slabs of what must be dried fish and long dark strips of dried meat.

When I run away I'll fill a sack with this stuff, Tomi told himself. How stupid they are! There isn't even a lock on the door. He realised, with a sudden lightening of his heart, that he wouldn't have to wait long enough to learn how to hunt

70

and make fire. He could leave whenever he chose. He strolled away from the storage house with a smile on his face.

By late afternoon the village was in a bustle. Steam and smoke rose in clouds from the cooking fires. The smells were mouthwatering. Tomi longed to order the women to bring him a plateful, but he kept quiet, sure that they would just snub him.

At last Swift walked into the centre of the glade and clapped his hands. "Eat and rejoice," he said. "For we are free."

"We are free," everyone echoed. Then they fell to. Today no one stopped Tomi from having as much as he wanted, so he ate until his stomach hurt. Oh, it felt good!

By the time the meal was over it was sunset and the forest was full of shadows. One of the smallest children was sent climbing into the topmost branches of a great tree that stood to the west of the glade. Tomi kept at the back of the crowd, puzzled, watching and listening. He tried to get Arbor to answer more questions, but Arbor just giggled and skipped away.

But he overheard Treefeller mutter to Swift, "What'll we do with *him*?"

"Don't worry. It's all taken care of," Swift whispered back.

Tomi moved quietly away, pretending not to have heard. What was all taken care of?

The small girl at the top of the tree shouted down. "It's time. The sun has gone behind the hill. It's time to start."

A man called Sage, the oldest, Tomi reckoned, judging by his white hair and beard, pulled a burning log from one of the cooking fires and thrust it into the heart of the great pile of wood that had been gathered in the middle of the glade. It smoked, crackled, and then took hold with a roar.

There was a great cheer. How much noise fifty people could make! Then they moved forward to gather about the new fire, leaving Tomi standing in the shadows. They all shared a cup, drank and spoke to each other. Then there was laughter and hugs and kisses.

71

Nobody ever held *me* like that, thought Tomi with a sudden pang.

What nonsense, he told himself firmly. After all, I am a Lord, not a savage. I don't need all that stuff. I have knowledge, and knowledge is power, and power is all the happiness I need.

But he was oddly grateful when Healhand came up to him with a cup in each hand and gave him one with a smile. "You must share our joy, Tomi." She drank to him and he in turn sipped the drink in his cup. It was sweet, but overlaid with a faint bitterness that lingered on his tongue after the sweetness had left.

"What are they saying to each other when they drink?" he asked.

"Oh... it is not important... something like... good health."

"Good health then." Tomi bowed formally, as if she were a lady and not a savage, and drained the cup. "What happens now?"

"Oh, dancing and singing and stories until the sun comes up. Why don't you sit comfortably over here where you can watch?" She threw some skins down on the ground in front of a smooth boulder. It was on the far side of the clearing from the fire, almost too far away to hear what was going on. But it did look very comfortable. He could rest for a while and later on walk closer if he wished to.

He settled back against the skins. The sky above the clearing darkened to a deep blue, almost black. He thought he could see the stars, but perhaps it was only sparks from the fire. It was huge, sending flickering light right across the clearing.

He could see the dark shapes of the savages as they formed a circle around the fire and began to dance around it. How hot they must be, he thought sleepily. Even across the clearing, with the cold forest at his back, he could feel the warmth of the flames. He settled against the furs. His eyes shut.

72

Afloat in a half dream of pleasant images, his stomach full for the first time since he had been hurled out of ArcOne, he heard snatches of a song, coming and going like a distant tide.

"The Lords' whips cracked till our backs were sore
... watched us bleed,
Till we swore we'd ...
Die or let's be freed.

Ay-di-doh, ay-di-doh dah-day
... ay-di-day-dee.
Now Devil-on-your back can't...
... will be free."

Tomi snored.

5
The Knife

TOMI swam sluggishly up through layers of sleep and forced his eyes open. He shut them again with a groan as a shaft of sunlight skewered through his brain. He became aware of a pounding inside his head behind the pain of the sunlight. He rolled over and sat up very carefully.

Why was the sun so bright? He opened his eyes again and looked blearily round. He was in the glade where he had sat last night to watch the dancing. He must have fallen asleep and they had let him lie there. He pushed aside a skin that had been thrown over him. It was wet with dew.

The glade was empty. Of the great fire nothing remained but a pile of white ash surrounded by a ring of blackened grass. The cooking fires were cold, and the doors of all the huts were shut. Yet the sun was high above the trees and the birds were shouting their heads off.

He got to his feet and staggered off in search of water. His head pounded unmercifully and there was an ugly taste in his mouth. He found a pot half full and drank from it greedily, pouring the rest over his head. That was a little better, though a bitter taste still lingered in his mouth.

Bitter taste! He remembereed the wine that Healhand had shared with him the night before. She had wished him good luck and smiled – and all the time the cup of wine had been drugged! Then he remembered the enigmatic conversation he had overheard between Treefeller and Swift.

"What'll we do with him?" Treefeller had asked.

"Don't worry. It's all taken care of," Swift had replied.

Taken care of! With an angry snort Tomi made for Swift's house. He would have it out with him right now. How dare they lie to him and drug him and prevent him from finding his way back to ArcOne. All right then! He tore open the door.

A faint snore curled up from the bed. He hesitated in the gloom, blinking to adjust his eyes from the brilliance outside. There on the right was the big bed where Swift and Healhand slept. On the left were two narrow cots, on the nearest of which Arbor slept. Tomi could just see the tousled top of his head among the skin rugs. Rowan lay beyond him neatly asleep on her back, her red hair tumbled across a folded fur skin tucked under her neck.

A gleam of light from the open shutter caught something bright and sent a sharp beam straight into Tomi's eyes. His head stabbed. He moved, so the light was no longer in his eyes, and looked down. There was Swift's knife, lying on top of his tunic on the rough chest that stood at the foot of the big bed.

He tiptoed forward, reached out and picked up the knife. I'll show him, he thought spitefully. The snoring stopped and he froze. In a minute there was a gentle sigh and the snoring began again. He backed slowly to the door, slipped through and closed it softly behind him. His heart was pounding as if he had been running hard. He took a deep breath and looked quickly round. No one stirred. The whole village still slept.

Tomi smiled. All he had to do was to find a safe place to hide the knife. Then he would pretend to be asleep and he wouldn't wake up until there were plenty of witnesses to his deep and drugged sleep. They would never think of blaming him. Swift would believe that he had just mislaid the knife.

Only where was the best place to hide it? His eyes scanned the clearing. He could think of no place where the others wouldn't think of looking. Beyond the circle of huts there was the forest. He could hide it there, but how would he be able to find it again? Hurry now. Think!

His eyes fell on the store room and he remembered. Roots. Dried fish. Berries. Meat...

Why shouldn't he leave *now*? He could take as much food as he could carry. With food and the knife he would survive in comfort. There would never be as good an opportunity. What had Healhand said? They would dance and tell stories until dawn. He glanced up at the sun. With luck they would sleep for hours yet.

He slipped into the storehouse. There was a handy grass basket with a long handle to slip over one shoulder. He filled it with dried fish and meat. He decided that roots were too heavy to carry and too unpleasant to eat raw. Too bad he hadn't found the secret of making fire yet. But he found a dish filled with flat cakes and he filled a second grass basket with these and slung it across his other shoulder. He tightened his sandal thongs, girded his toga around him and turned his back on the village.

He went north. Though the savages had told him repeatedly that ArcOne did not lie on the river he had no reason to believe that they were telling the truth; after all, they had deceived him in so many other ways.

At first he stayed close to the river, afraid of losing his way. There were rapids to look for: two sets of them, perhaps more. It was hard to remember all the details of his nightmare trip down river. By then he should be able to see the dam and spillway spanning the river. And the Dome.

But close to the river there were many fallen trees and a tangle of new growth around them. Walking was almost impossible. Further away from the river the trees were bigger, and set far enough apart for some grass to establish itself between them. He wasn't risking much by leaving the river bank. He could still hear the water, and surely its changing voice would warn him that he was approaching the rapids.

He slugged on, scrambling up hills, occasionally descending into gentle declines, some of them watered by streams that flowed from east to west into the big river. There were none that he could not cross in a single stride. Always the land rose ahead of him.

The sun flickered through the trees on his right, dancing from light to shade and back again in a pattern that made his aching head uneasy. He tried to ignore it. Soon the sun will be behind me as noon approaches, he told himself. But no matter how long he went on walking the sun still shone over his right shoulder, only now it was higher in the sky.

He stopped and thought about it. He listened. Yes, there was the song of the river over to his left. He had made no mistake. So why wasn't the sun on his back by now? He consulted his infopaks.

– Perhaps you are travelling in a path that curves towards the east – his infopak suggested.

He tried to remember. Had the river done that? He thought not. He turned to his left and slid downhill until he was just above the river. It flowed smooth and clear amber. He could see its speed only in the tugging ripple at the reeds close to its edge. He could see the shadowy forms of great fish lurking under boulders. *His* river hadn't looked like this. *His* river had been white and wild.

He stared across at the opposite bank, a gentle slope covered with leafy trees. *His* river had had a wall of dark rock broken into vertical cracks like pillars, and the trees were needled and dark, not soft and leafy green and gold.

The wrong river! They hadn't lied to him after all. He had followed the wrong river. For how long? Where had he got off track? His knees gave way and he collapsed against a tree trunk. He wiped his sweating face with a corner of his toga and tried to think logically.

After a while he picked up a twig and scratched in the dirt beneath the tree the course of his river as far as he could recall it, from the wild trip down the rapids to the widening, where he had been suddenly buffeted by an unexpected current and almost lost his hold on the log. It was not long after that that the river had turned west

77

around a bulge of land and then turned east again a little above the place where he had drifted ashore on the island. So far so good.

He had gone ashore and followed the river back to the bulge, where he had taken a shortcut over the hilly meadow to the place where he had gone back to the river to drink. Then he had walked some more, eaten the poison berries, and been taken... where? Not far; Rowan couldn't have dragged him far.

He stared at the scratches in the dirt. They didn't make sense...

Another river, he suddenly thought. A river flowing south-westward from the right of the col to join *his* river above the bulge in the land. That would be the place where the river had widened and the sudden current nearly upset him. Yes, that made sense. And by taking a shortcut across the bulge he had missed the confluence and taken for granted that he was following the same river.

He groaned and dropped his head to his knees. Was all his walking for nothing? And what was he to do now? He daren't go back, not after taking their food and their knife.

He looked up and stared across the river with sudden hope. ArcOne was probably due west of where he sat now. Across this river, over the hill, along the ridge of the col and up the next mountain. Could he cross the river? It was too deep to wade. Too wide to risk swimming. Besides, if he got his food wet it would spoil, and he had no idea how long it would take him to reach ArcOne. He accessed his infopaks.

If a river is too wide and too deep to ford, how can I cross it without a boat?

– Go upstream. Eventually the river will become small enough for you to cross.

How long will that take?

– Insufficient data. Input map please.

If I had a map! He stopped and suddenly thought how silly it was to be arguing with his own head. He felt tired and very reluctant to start walking again. Perhaps a meal, he thought, and ate a handful of berries and couple of flat cakes.

When he had finished them he got doggedly to his feet and began to walk. Evidently the river he was following was still veering to the east, so that every painful step took him further and further from ArcOne. He could no longer see the col between the two mountains that had been his landmark. There was only a low hill on the other side of the river, and beyond it a mountain.

How strange that it should have snow on it at this time of year. It must be much higher than it looked. Or *was* that snow, that tiny lens-shaped blob near the top? *Near* the top. Not *at* the top.

Tomi strained his eyes and tried to straighten his stooped shoulders, as if he could see that much more by stretching another five centimetres. If only he could climb a tree and get a decent view. It didn't seem to be difficult. That small female savage had swarmed up the big tree the night before as if it were nothing at all.

He looked around for the perfect tree, one with a sturdy trunk and branches evenly spaced. When he found it he told himself that it was really not much different from climbing a ladder, more secure in fact. Though of course he had never climbed a ladder either. That was for slaves or workers, not for Lords.

He slipped the food baskets from his shoulders, untied the thongs of his sandals and kicked them off. He took Swift's knife from his waistband and laid it carefully down on one of the baskets. Then he spat on his hands as the little girl had done, rubbed his palms against his sides and set his hands and feet to the great tree.

The first few steps were the most difficult as the branches, though sturdy, were far apart. Sweating and grunting, he struggled up. Whenever he had to straighten to reach the branch above, the infopaks pulled painfully at the sockets in his neck. But the further he climbed, the closer together were the branches and the easier it became. Soon

79

Tomi found he was getting the knack of climbing quite nicely.

It was exciting too, in a way that was hard to describe. His face was running with sweat, but up here there was a light breeze that freshened him and dried the sweat. Now he was above the lesser trees, seeing as a bird must see. And he had done it himself, without help, with his own weak and flabby body. Why, this was a thousand times more exciting than Dreamland, where only your mind faced the hazards.

He had a wild longing to climb up to the very topmost branches, but his logical mind told him not to be so foolish. He was here for one purpose only.

He stood on a smooth branch, his bare toes curled downwards to grip it, his arms over the next branch. Looking westwards over a flattish area, which must be the lower slopes of the col, he could see the mountain, the trees straggling up its steep sides until at last they gave up. The summit was bare. He could see no white glint. His heart sank with disappointment. He had really thought that maybe... but it had just been his eyes playing tricks.

His eyes drifted down the left flank of the mountain. If his arms had not been across the branch he might well have fallen. As it was he started, his foot slipped and he hung, wildly kicking, until he was able to get his feet safely back. There, unmistakable, its dome rounded by the light of the golden afternoon sun, was ArcOne.

He tried to estimate how far away it was. He put out his arm and reckoned the distance from his hand to his eye at the moment when the width of his thumb covered the whole dome from side to side. Then he accessed trigonometry and reckoned that ArcOne could not be more than twelve kilometres away.

As the missile flies, he reminded himself. On foot it would be another story. But not more than a day's walk away, surely. Not more than a day.

Eager to start he looked down to find a foothold on the branch below. He gulped. The tree that had seemed so solid as he had climbed up now looked like a reed narrowing to a point on the ground far far below. From the narrow reed the branches stuck out like the spokes of a wheel. As he stared down in horrified fascination the spokes began to turn, to revolve faster and faster. Then the whole earth lifted and turned beneath him. Above his head the sky too moved. The whole earth was hurtling through space at impossible speeds and he was going to be torn from his perch and flung outward.

Tomi shut his eyes and clung to the branch, his cheek grazing the bark. He swallowed nausea and groaned. How was he going to be able to climb down? He could never do it. Never.

After a long time he forced the stiff fingers of one hand to loosen their grip on the branch. Clinging to the trunk he slowly lowered himself to his knees until he could grasp the branch he had been standing on. Then there was the heartstopping moment of letting his legs slide and hang free in space until his bare toes could find the next lowest branch. And over again. And again. He wouldn't look down. I am a Lord, he told himself. And I will behave like a Lord.

When he was absolutely sure that he must be close enough to the ground to let go and slide free, he dared to look down again. The ground seemed as far away as ever! Yet climbing up had been so very easy. He could have wept, but he gritted his teeth together and went on with the slow painful descent. Finally his bare feet touched dead leaves. He let his tired arms go and fell, his face among the cool bitter-smelling leaves.

After a while he sat up and wiped the sweat and dirt off his face with the corner of his toga. He slipped on his sandals and tied them carefully. Then he got to his feet with a groan. Muscles he did not even know existed knotted his calves into pain. He stooped to pick up the baskets and looked around for the knife. He had laid it most carefully on top of the basket that had held the meat and fish. Had it fallen into the grass?

He knelt down and searched. He emptied the precious

food onto the ground and shook out the bags before repacking them. He looked through the grass again, combing it with frantic fingers, turning over fallen leaves, in an ever widening circle around the base of the tree. But the knife had vanished.

He stood up slowly and turned. There in the shadows Swift and Treefeller stood watching him. He began to run, instinctively, hopelessly. Swift was on him before he had taken two paces.

"No! Let me go!" He bent and bit the hairy arm and tasted blood. He exalted in his anger and kicked at Swift's legs. Swift hooked a hard foot around his ankle and sent him head first into the grass.

"So that's how lordlings behave these days!" Swift examined the toothmarks in his arm, seeming to be amused rather than angry. He sucked the wound and spat out blood. Tomi wriggled to one side and tried to get to his knees, but Treefeller's large foot was on his shoulder blades, pressing his face into the dirt.

"You could lose your arm with a bite from filth like this," Treefeller grumbled. "Make sure you get it cleaned back home."

Swift only laughed. He squatted beside Tomi. "I'll give you a choice, which is more than you deserve. You can walk back with us, like a Lord, with your promise not to escape. Or you'll be carried."

"I'll make you no promises." It was difficult to sound dignified with his face pressed into the grass, but Tomi did his best.

Swift did not waste time arguing. Tomi's ankles were lashed together. He was pulled to his feet and his hands were bound in front of him. Then, with no more effort than if he were a bundle of dried grass, he was thrown over Treefeller's broad shoulder.

He made the journey back to the village upside down, bouncing gently with Treefeller's easy stride. The blood rushing to his head did not improve his temper, nor did Treefeller's exclamation as he was dumped on the grass in front of the huts. "Phew, we should starve this barrel of lard for a moon or two. I've hefted deer that were lighter."

Tomi landed face down in the grass. He wriggled over onto his side, to see two slender brown ankles close to his forehead. He looked up into Rowan's angry face.

"What a horrible thing to do! How could you?"

"I'd every right to leave if I chose, especially after the way you treated me."

"Huh?"

"Drugging my wine."

"Oh, that. Well, Healhand had to do it. You don't understand."

"I had to leave. You'd no right to stop me."

"But to take the *knife*!"

"I needed it."

"So did we. It is the only one we have."

He blushed and muttered. "Well, I wasn't to know that, was I? Undo me, can't you?"

She drew back. "That's up to Swift."

He tried to smile. "But I thought we were friends."

She looked at him sternly. "You don't know *anything* about being friends." She walked away and he was alone.

The sun slid down between the trees, and the cooking fires were blown into life. Tomi was ignored. Slowly, by twos and threes, the villagers came drifting in from the forest or the meadow. Each person had something to add to the store of food: a basket of roots or berries, a string slung with fish, a couple of birds, a rabbit.

Each returning person was welcomed by the others with a hug or a kiss. Savages, thought Tomi, unnoticed in the shadows. Why, his parents, the Lord and Lady Bentt, would never even touch each other in public, much less *kiss*. And nobody had ever hugged *him* that he could remember.

He suddenly remembered the morning of Accession Day, when he had been so nervous and Seventy-Three had reached out and gently squeezed his foot. Had that really been the most loving moment of his life: the touch of a slave? He pushed the thought out of his mind. Just savages, he told himself firmly.

The sun set in a welter of incredible reds. How strange it must be to live above ground all your life and see this magnificence every clear evening. But of course it would be wasted on these people. They would be used to it and probably had little feelings for beauty anyway.

Then he noticed that though everyone was busy, fetching wood, stirring the pots, cutting up meat, they would stop now and then, straighten their backs and stand looking into the western sky. Sometimes they would reach out to touch someone else, and they too would stop and look.

Tears ran hot and painful down Tomi's cheeks. His chest hurt and he held his bound hands against it, hunching his legs so that his thighs were pressed against his front. Never in all his fourteen years had he felt so lonely or so insignificant.

A kindly hand touched his shoulder. He looked up, bleary-eyed, into Swift's concerned face. "Forgive me. I should not have left you alone so long. If I untie you do I have your word that you will not run away?"

Tomi hesitated. He couldn't bear being outcast any more, but a promise like that?

"... before morning," added Swift.

Tomi nodded and held out his hands to be untied. Swift rolled up the grass twine and stowed it carefully in one of the pockets of his tunic. Then he bent to Tomi's ankles. In the struggle the knot had tightened. Swift had trouble with it.

"Can't you use your knife?"

"And waste a good piece of twine? Patience. It's coming."

As he bent over Tomi's feet his hair, sun-bleached to the colour of dry grass, parted and fell forward. Tomi had the strange feeling that he had been in this position before and would see the same thing. He looked down and saw the

84

five centimetre line of puckered scar tissue that ran across the nape of Swift's neck. He gasped and drew back his foot.

"Hold still. I almost have it. There." Swift wound the twine around the flat of his hand and tucked the loose end in. He looked up with a smile that faded as he saw the expression on Tomi's face. "What's the matter. Are you ill?"

"You're a *slave*. You're a runaway slave from ArcOne! Why, you all are, aren't you?" he guessed, and saw from Swift's face that he was right.

Swift got to his feet in a single graceful movement. He looked down at Tomi. "I am no slave. I am free. Free to live, to love, to be at peace with this beautiful land. Can you say as much, New Lord Tomi of Bentt?"

He held out his hand to help Tomi to his feet as he spoke, but Tomi brushed his hand aside and scrambled clumsily up, groaning at the stiffness in his knees. "I saw ArcOne on the mountain over there. No more than a day's journey across the river. You lied to me, number whatever-you-are. You should be whipped."

"None of us has lied to you. We told you that ArcOne was not on our river."

"You deliberately deceived me."

"Yes. We did not trust you. We would have told you in time, when you had become one of us."

"One of *you*."

The contempt in Tomi's voice brought a flush of anger to Swift's cheeks, though his voice and eyes were steady. "Yes, we would have asked you to join us in time."

"And you would have told me that you are slaves?"

"*Were* slaves. Not any more. Yes, we would have told you that too. You would have become a part of our dance and our story."

How would Father behave in his place, Tomi asked himself. It was important to show right away who was boss, that was it. He pushed past Swift and walked towards the centre of the clearing. Standing by the cooking fire he began to talk, and everyone turned to look at him. He was a ridiculous figure, his fat body swathed in his torn and dirty toga, but in his voice was the authority of one who had always been obeyed.

"I demand to be escorted back to ArcOne." His voice broke shrilly into the soft conversations. "Those who return with me will be accepted back without severe punishment. Those who do not..." He swung round, his hands on his fat hips. "They will be hunted down by the soldiers and killed. You are slaves, you are the property of the City. You had no right to leave."

Some of the small children began to cry, more at his tone than at the meaning of his words. A few people bent to hush them, to pick them up and comfort them. The rest stood straight and still in the flickering light from the fires. Their faces were blank with shock.

Then the shock was replaced by anger. They began to move towards Tomi. One man bent to pick up a flint scraper that had been dropped beside a half-cleaned skin. Seeing his movement Groundsel reached for a stone.

"Stop!" Swift's voice was like the first crack of thunder in the silence before a storm. People jumped. Some stopped. Some continued to move closer to Tomi. Swift pushed through the crowd.

"Look at him. He's a fat foolish boy, nothing more."

"He could destroy all of us, Swift. We've got to get rid of him."

"He can only hurt us if he gets back to ArcOne. And for tonight he has given his word not to escape."

"The word of a Lord?" The scorn in the voice whipped the blood into Tomi's cheeks. He opened his mouth, but Swift dropped a casual hand to his shoulder and squeezed it with fingers of iron.

"He should not be held responsible for the sins of his fathers. He has promised."

"A promise to slaves?" Treefeller's voice was mocking.

Tomi, who had just been thinking that a promise to slaves didn't really count and that as soon as everyone was asleep he should make a run for it, flushed indignantly. "My word is good!"

"So be it!" Treefeller's words were more than a simple acknowledgement. Somehow Tomi had hit on a phrase that was important to these people. The men drew back. Groundsel dropped the stone. The man with the flint scraper put it back by the rabbit skin.

Swift held up his hand. "Wait. Listen. Tomi is very young. He's lived his whole life as a Lord, learning to think like a Lord. He has accessed considerable *knowledge*. He is not stupid. It is time that he learned some *wisdom*. I ask for a Sharing."

"Sharing!" There was a shocked silence and then a clamour of voices.

Swift's quiet voice overrode them. "Listen to me, sisters and brothers. I agree that Tomi is a danger to us all. But not because of what he *knows*. Because of what he does not know. If we leave him in ignorance we never dare let him go. But we can't watch him every moment of his life. And we cannot kill him. We are not soldiers!"

Healhand spoke first. "Swift is right. I vote to share."

"So do I then, if you agree."

"And I."

"Oh, very well then, so do I."

One by one each man and woman came forward and held up a hand, palm forward.

"Why not you?" Tomi asked Rowan. "Aren't you going to vote to share with me, whatever that is?"

"I am freeborn, not freefound. I have nothing to share." She turned away and ran after the others. Tomi turned to Swift. "I don't understand."

"In time it will all become clear. As soon as we have eaten and lit the great fire you will listen to our Sharing and then you will understand." Swift's voice was heavy, and Tomi felt a sense of dread that made no sense at all. After all, what could be bad about Sharing? Whatever Sharing was...

6
The Sharing

THE NIGHT BEFORE had been a joyful feast; tonight everyone ate in silence. When the great fire was lit no one cheered except for a couple of small boys who began to dance around it until they were caught and distracted with a handful of sweet berries.

As on the night before a cup of wine was shared. When it was offered to him Tomi hesitated. "Yesterday we had a heavy secret to keep from you. It is a secret no more. We are Sharing, so please drink."

Tomi looked into the steady eyes of the slave who called herself Healhand. For a moment he felt a warmth. . . then he shook his head and pushed away the hand that offered the cup.

When all but Tomi had drunk, Swift shook the few drops that remained onto the ground. "We are one with each other and with our Mother the Earth. We are one in our freedom. Let us rejoice in our freedom and our oneness!"

Everyone linked hands until they circled the fire. They moved to the left and back to the right, and as they danced they sang a song that Tomi felt he had heard before, only in a dream:

> "The Lords' whips cracked till our backs were sore
> And the Three-eyes watched us bleed,
> Till we swore we'd not work any more —
> Die or let's be freed.

So the Freedom Man danced out of the Arc,
Over the hills so shady,
Into the light and out of the dark,
With his long-haired lady.

Now we're free to think and free to grow
Under the sky so blue,
Down in the fields where the flowers blow,
Part of a world made new.

Ay-di-doh, ay-di-doh dah-day
Ay-di-doh, ay-di-day-dee.
Now Devil-on-your-back can't make you pay
And your children will be free. "

The song stopped and the dancers dropped back to sit in a wide circle around the fire. The flames flickered up and a log broke in a shower of sparks, showing the red heart of the fire. No one spoke. They watched the flames, watched the red heart of the fire.

Tomi had stood outside the circle of dancers, but when they fell back to sit around the fire he found that whether he chose to or not he was now part of the circle. The quietness, broken only by the crackle of the burning wood, worked its way into the angry centre of his being. He found himself staring, his eyes drawn to the heart of the fire, seeing in the shape of the glowing logs the passages and rooms of ArcOne.

A piece of bark flamed and twisted into a shape of pain: Grog screaming and fighting against the insertion of his infopaks. A log fell away and in its crimson heart he saw the pool of blood at the foot of the altar, and once again the kitchen filled with slaves and a smell of hate stronger even than the smell of garbage.

He shivered and shut his eyes. There was some kind of evil magic in the fire. He wouldn't look into it any more. They couldn't make him. It was all a trick. Frantically he began to fill his mind with noise...

– The rare earths are lanthanum, cerium, prasodymium . . .
At the centre of the earth the pressure reaches 3 million
atmospheres . . . The central temperature of the sun is 6,000
million degrees Kelvin –

A voice close to Tomi spoke into the silence of the dying
fire. "In the beginning was the Age of Oil. Then there was no
more oil. The scientists could travel to the planets, probe the
mysteries of the universe; but they could not turn back the
clock. It had taken tens of millions of years for the oil to be
formed and it was all used up in a hundred and fifty years,
squandered on joy-rides and plastic gadgetry." The words
were formal, as if learned by heart and passed down from
father to son, mother to daughter. In spite of the fire's heat
Tomi felt his skin crawl.

Another voice from across the circle took up the story.
"The Arab States collapsed with the last of the oil in 2005
A.D. Then followed the Age of Confusion."

It was not precisely dark. The remains of the fire glowed
red, casting an unreal shimmer over the cheekbones of the
people seated around it, now and then reflecting a red spark
in someone's eye. But the rest was shadow and it was out of
this shadow that the voices spoke, to tell a story that was like,
and yet different from, the history that Tomi had learned
from his infopaks.

"There was starvation and people died. There were
riots for food and for jobs and more people died. Gov-
ernments were no longer able to keep order. In the cities
the old diseases began to come back, diseases almost un-
recognized except from history books: polio, cholera, the
plague."

Another voice continued. "It was no longer safe to live in
cities; but families living on farms were not safe either,
because as soon as food distribution within the cities broke
down, gangs began to sweep the countryside looking for
what they could take. Radio and TV stations were wrecked
during the riots or the fires that followed, so there was no
communication. Each small part of the nation had to make its

90

own rules and its own plan for survival. One such plan was ArcOne..."

"ArcOne was a magnificent dream." Was that Healhand's voice taking up the thread of the story? Tomi peered into the shadows, but he could not tell. The fire shimmered, a bed of cherry red charcoal. Above it a moonless sky burned with stars.

"It began at the University. The professors said: 'We must save knowledge, as the monks saved it during the dark ages in old Europe. We will ride out the storm and preserve in computers the whole knowledge of our culture until the Age of Confusion is over and we can begin to rebuild'."

Healhand, if it were she, stopped talking. After a moment's silence a man continued. "Everyone worked together, secretly digging down into the mountain an underground city, a kilometre in diameter. Everyone's hands poured the concrete. Everyone took it in turn to wrestle the generator into place. Everyone helped to erect the Dome and circle the City with an electric fence. Everyone shared in the work and everyone had time over for more learning."

There was a heavy silence. A small chill wind licked the dying charcoal into momentary flame. Then a sigh ran round the circle no louder than the wind. Tomi shivered. He wanted to get up and run into the forest, no matter how dark and threatening it might be. He wanted most desperately *not* to hear the rest of the story. At the same time he knew he *had* to know.

Another voice broke the oppressive silence. "Then came the darkest night in ArcOne's history, the shameful night when a small group of scientists decided that it would be better if they could spend their entire energies on scientific studies, leaving those who were perhaps less successful to the work of looking after the City. They divided the population into what later came to be known as Lords and Workers. No choice was offered, no vote taken. They

91

designed the infopaks and grafted them onto all the people of ArcOne. What a gift! To be linked to the Central Computer, to access all the knowledge of Earth!"

Tomi nodded in agreement. He felt a glow of pride inside him. Yes, the paks were a marvellous gift.

"Only it was a lie!" A harsh voice close to Tomi broke in. Though the face was shadowed he recognized the gnarled hands of Treefeller. "Each person got carefully selected information, and each was taught to be completely happy with what he got. In this way the workers, whether they were running the generator, tilling the Dome gardens or working in the kitchens, were content with what they were doing, and felt they were superior to every other class of worker."

What's wrong with that? thought Tomi. What better way to run a city than by making sure that everyone is happy? He was just about to say so when a woman beyond Treefeller spoke.

"Only there was a flaw in the scheme. In time a new class of people grew up in the City, those whose bodies rejected the input socket graft. These people were not in contact with the Computer at all, and though they were ignorant, they could see the Great Lie for what it was. How could the Lords deal with *that* threat? They called them slaves, these people with no knowledge, no rights, no Sharing. But because the slaves had one precious thing that the workers did not – free will – the Lords had to design a new class of citizen, computer trained for only one job. To keep the slaves in order. Soldiers. Two soldiers for every slave in the city. Once more the City was stable and at peace."

A woman's voice sang out of the darkness:

"The Lords' whips cut till our backs were sore
And the Three-eyes watched us bleed..."

In the silence that followed Tomi fought anger and disbelief. But there was worse to come.

92

"So the new classless society, designed to save civilization, now had four classes: Lords, workers, soldiers and slaves. One hundred and forty years have gone by since those days and the balance has never changed in spite of births and deaths. There are still twelve thousand people in ArcOne: three thousand Lords, six thousand workers, two thousand soldiers and a thousand slaves. How strange that the proportion should never change! Or is it? One man is Overlord of the Computer. It is his choice who is to be Lord or worker or soldier. Even sometimes who shall be slave. What began as a medical problem of rejection is now a deliberate part of the system."

"That's a black lie!" Tomi tried to get to his feet, but the two men on either side of him forced him down. "Do you think we wouldn't find out about it, we Lords? We're equal. We share all knowledge. Why, that is the honour of being a Lord."

"Honour?" asked a voice. "*Honour?*" In its quietness was so much anger and disgust that Tomi shrank back, shaking.

"Shall we speak of the honour of a Lord who can say: This man is to be brainwashed to spy and even to kill; this man will be a worker happily thinking he is better than anyone else; this Lord will think he has complete access . . . think of the honour of a man who has bound everyone to the computer except himself. What a City! One man free at the top and a thousand slaves free at the bottom! And not one of you has ever guessed that one man and only one man controls the Computer, because he has never allowed you to guess. But we *knew*, we at the bottom too stupid for the Computer to brainwash."

"It's a lie!"

"Lord Tomi of Bentt, think for yourself for once in your young life. Think about the possibility of there being one Lord who does not sleep when sleep is ordained for all, who is already awake when the Computer wakes the City. But of course you could never guess. You were asleep. Only the slaves were not."

A Lord who did not sleep when the others did... a nagging suspicion slid uninvited into Tomi's mind. He thrust it out, but it crept back. He remembered that no matter how quickly he rose in the morning he never seemed to catch his father unprepared, unshaved, or waiting in line for the shower.

"Aren't you curious to know the name of the Lord who has held this power over the people of ArcOne for the last twenty years?"

"No, I don't. I'm not interested. I don't believe..."

"You *have* guessed, haven't you? It is the Lord Bentt who is now the Overlord of ArcOne."

It was necessary, Tomi told himself wildly. The City had to maintain the correct population, maintain order, maintain...

With unnerving clarity he suddenly saw the mad face of Farfat as his brain rejected the infopaks that would have made him a Lord. He could hear Grog's screams of agony as his socket refused to accept the inplant. He remembered wondering if it were luck, as he and Denn had walked away thankful of their newly acquired honours. Luck!

"I know you will succeed," Lord Bentt had said to him on Access morning. Tomi had thought that he meant he believed in his only son. But he hadn't meant that at all. He had *known*. The system had been rigged so that Grog and Farfat should fail and the son of the precious House of Bentt should succeed.

> *"Now we're free to think and free to grow*
> *Under the sky so blue."*

The soft singing seemed to mock his agony.

I'll never be free, not till I'm dead, thought Tomi, and "Farfat, Grog, I'm sorry!" he screamed. Then he plunged out of the circle of firelight so quickly that he was gone before they could stop him.

He had no notion of where he was going. He wanted only to escape from the people who knew his shame, who had

94

known it from the first moment he had so proudly given his name. Before, when Tomi had run from the village, he had been running *home*. Now he had no home, no place to run to. Only away.

His feet ran on. His hands warded off branches that whipped close to his face. He went downhill towards a gleam of silvery light. He broke out of the trees and saw it was the image of the moon newly risen above the hill, lying on the dark water of the river, a shimmering pure whiteness.

To fall into that whiteness, to be lost in it forever and to forget, seemed to be the most natural thing in the world to do. Without engaging his will or his brain Tomi let his feet carry him down the hill, across the shingle and into the water. It accepted him, pulled him down into itself, wrapped him in darkness...

His breathing reflex forced his diaphragm down. His lungs sucked in water. His arms and legs thrashed wildly and he broke through the blackness into silver moonlight, choking and spitting. He fought desperately to keep his head up in the white light, away from the black. He was moving down river, but the whiteness seemed to move with him.

Then it vanished. For a second, silhouetted against the moonlit sky, Tomi saw the outline of a dead and leafless tree. He went under, touched bottom, came up again. His knees and elbows were rubbing against rough wetness. Then his face was in slime and his hands were clutching the knife-sharp sedge.

For a long time Tomi lay with his cheek in the slime, his face turned to the right just enough so that he could breathe. Now and then he coughed spasmodically. After a while he began to shiver.

Much later on he felt a whiteness against his closed lids and he opened his eyes and rolled as far onto his back as he could. Above him the moon floated serenely on the clear night, a lens-shaped curve, past the full.

> *"Slowly, silently, now the moon*
> *Walks the night in her silver shoon."*

How strange the moon was. He felt as if it held some secret knowledge, if only...

He reached out for wisdom and his infopak cut in with a rush of information: the moon's average distance from the earth is 384,000 kilometres, its diameter is 3476 kilometres and its surface gravity is..."

"Stop it. I don't want to hear that. Stop it! Shut up." Tomi struggled to his knees and, grunting with pain, reached over his shoulder to the nape óf his neck and pulled each infopak from its socket. Lastly he pulled out his lifepak. He threw them aside and remained for some time on his knees with his head bent, panting and sweating, his mind wiped clean.

"Yes," he remembered at last and fell backwards to the grass, his arms outflung. "Oh, yes, that is better."

He lay flat on his back, unimpeded by his paks, while the moon silently showered him with silver light, buried him in mountains of light. Yet no matter how much light it poured on him there seemed to be as much left. That was terribly important to remember, he told himself, happily...

7
Welcome Back

HE SIGHED and looked drowsily up into the rafters of a house. Those are trees, he told himself. Trees grow in forests, was his next thought. And then, some time later: I am in a house made of trees in the middle of a forest. He stretched, wriggled his toes and went back to sleep.

When he next awoke he was hungry. Part of him wanted to get out of bed and open the door, find someone who would give him something to eat. The other part of him wanted to go on lying just as he was, totally relaxed. He decided in favour of being lazy and lay enjoying the pleasure of knowing he was being lazy.

The door swung open to an oblong of greenish-gold light and a shadowy figure. He looked with pleasure at the strange woman with fair sun-bleached hair and brown skin. She was holding a bowl and a wooden spoon.

"Welcome back," she said with a smile. "You have been asleep for days. You must be hungry. Can you manage to sit up?"

He struggled up on his elbows and stared at her. "I know you, don't I? I've met you before?"

She looked at him closely and then smiled. "Yes. My name is Healhand. You've been ill, but you are better now. Drink this broth and sleep some more. When you wake up you will be quite well."

She fed him spoonful by spoonful as if he were an infant. Obediently he opened his mouth and then swallowed the delicious soup and smiled at her because he felt so happy he

97

just had to smile. And she smiled back. When he had finished he wiped his mouth with the back of his hand, burped contentedly and slid back under the fur covers.

His next awakening was into darkness. He was frightened and wanted to call someone, but he had no memory of names to call. 'Mom' had the right kind of sound, but something told him that it wouldn't do. Then a voice spoke in his memory: "You have been ill, but now you are better. When you wake up you will be quite well."

He repeated the words in the darkness and remembered who had spoken them: Healhand. Now he had a name he was no longer afraid. Just before his eyes shut he thought of another question: Who am *I*? What is *my* name? But he fell asleep before he had found the answer.

He awoke to daylight and an urgent need to relieve himself. He staggered out of bed and found that under the fur coverings he was naked. He wrapped a skin around himself and opened the door. There was sun and a smell of woodsmoke and a bite in the air that made his skin shiver, but not unpleasantly. Smiling faces turned to him, and a man came forward from the fire and showed him the way to the clean little house set back among the trees.

When he came out the man was waiting for him with a tunic and breeches of soft skin. Soon he was warm and the goosebumps on his arms went away. He was shown a place by the fire and given a bowl of warm mush to eat. It was very good. He didn't look up from the bowl until he had finished every scrap. Then he set the bowl down carefully on the grass and looked around.

There were children playing in the glade, dodging from stump to stump. Their happy laughter made him laugh too. Then everyone smiled.

"How are you today?" The woman called Healhand bent over him.

"I feel..." He took a deep breath of cool fresh air, felt the warmth of the mush settling in his stomach. "I feel wonderful."

98

"I am very glad. We all are. Tomi, I must..."

"What did you say?" A dark shadow hovered at the edge of the sunny glade of his happiness. "What was that name?"

"*Tomi*. What's the matter? Why are you looking like that?"

"Please don't say that name. He... Tomi, you know..." He whispered the name. "He's bad. You don't want him here. Please don't talk about him again."

She took both his hands in hers. "It's all right. We won't talk about him. It's all right, don't worry."

She left him to tell the others not to say that name. He began to feel better. The sun shone again and the shadow vanished. Four children raced by and lay on their fronts behind a big tree stump.

"Can I play too?" he asked. "Can I?"

"Sssh! Don't talk to us. Don't look this way or he'll know we're here," a small girl hissed.

"Who will?"

"Him." She pointed to a boy standing facing a tree across the glade. "He's the Lord and we're the slaves. We've got to get home free before he catches us. Now shush!" She dropped to the ground as the boy turned from the tree.

"Ready or not I've come from the Arc
To catch you all and put you in the dark!"

the boy shouted, and began to run.

The colours in the glade darkened and he shivered and looked up, expecting to see a cloud in front of the sun, but the sky was blue and cloudless. He put his hands to his face.

Outside the dark turmoil of his mind he could hear the excited screams and laughter of the children. A soft hand patted his cheek. "It's all right. It's all right."

He looked up. The small girl stood beside him. "You don't have to be afraid," she told him. "It's only a game. We're all free here. The Lords'll never find us."

He shivered and could say nothing.

"D'you want to play with us? You can if you want."

99

"N... no, thank you," he managed to stammer. His face felt stiff and hard like baked clay. She kissed his cheek and ran off to join her friends, turning at the edge of the glade to wave before disappearing into the shadows. He could feel where she had touched his cheek, but distantly, as if she had kissed him through some thick shell or husk that surrounded him.

Healhand came back. "You look tired. Would you like to rest?"

"Yes. Yes, I think I would."

She walked beside him to the little house that was his very own place, and he went inside thankfully. It was dim and chilly, still holding the cold of the night and Healhand left the door open when she went away. He lay on his back on the furs that covered the bed and wondered what was happening to him. Who was he? Who had he been? He felt almost not there, like a moth or a cobweb.

After he had rested for a little while he got up and began to wander around the little house. There was not much to see. Four walls of horizontal logs chinked with clay. A packed dirt floor. Rafters holding up a roof of thin logs and split shingles.

There were two beds, his and one that seemed to be unused, and at the bottom of each bed a chest, made from a sawed-off section of log painstakingly hollowed out. He lifted the curved lid of the one at the foot of the other bed, marvelling at its smoothness and the way the lid fitted so neatly, with leather hinges at the back and a leather strap that fastened over a wooden knob in front.

The chest held nothing but folded furs. He looked at them and then let the lid fall. It made a hollow sound that echoed the hollow feeling inside his head. There was something he had to do. Something he didn't want to.

He walked slowly to the foot of *his* bed and slipped the leather strap off the knob of the second chest. He let the lid fall back against the bed and looked inside...

Nothing to be afraid of. Some pieces of torn cloth, hardly

100

worth saving. When he picked them up he could feel that the material was some flimsy slippery stuff with no warmth in it. There was a shirt. A pair of undershorts. A long straight piece with a coloured border along one edge. He looked at the border. Funny. When he didn't think about it too much it almost seemed that the design meant something, as if it were in writing. But as soon as he stared at it the meaning dissolved into an abstract pattern... After a while he let the piece of cloth fall to the ground. He was so tired.

There was something else in the chest. A pile of oblong things... smaller than the palm of his hand... like... he didn't know what they were like... made of something... the name was on the tip of his tongue.

He picked up one of them and turned it over in his hand. Just an oblong box. He tried to open it, but it resisted his fingers. At one end was a sticking out piece with dozens of tiny rods... connections... to fit into a socket, memory suddenly told him. He dropped the box with a clatter and his hands went to the back of his neck. It was covered with a bandage, a dressing, something. It hurt when he pressed it.

Images danced across his brain like the spirally dancing insects in the sunlight caught between trees. A door suddenly swung open into the darkness at the back of his mind.

"That is Tomi."

He slammed the lid of the chest, saw the clothing on the floor, snatched it up and bundled it back and shut the lid once more.

Quick. Quick. His hands were so clumsy, his fingers fumbling to push the leather flap over the fastening knob. There! Now he was safe. Safe as long as he could keep Tomi shut up inside the chest. But it was scary being in the same room. He didn't want to sleep there any more, knowing what was in the chest at the foot of the bed.

He ran outside, shivering. There was sunshine, and a man stopped and put an arm around his shoulders. It felt good. Memory tickled. "Do I know you?"

101

"Yes. My name is Swift. Why are you frightened?"

"It's him... Tomi. He's..." He jerked his head to show where. He daren't point in case Tomi was watching, peering through the slit between the chest and the lid. "In there," he whispered. "*You* know."

"Won't you show me?"

"No! We mustn't let him out. He's bad. If he got out he'd hurt us. Remember? '*Ready or not I've come from the Arc to catch you all and put you in the dark.*'"

He began to cry, and the man called Swift turned him so that his head was buried against Swift's shoulder. Arms held him tightly. "Get Healhand," a voice said urgently.

That was good. Healhand will help. She had always helped, from when you first ate the poison berries... What poison berries?

You were hungry, remember? he told himself. You'd been trapped on the island for two days and then you walked upriver looking for the way back to the... to the... the City. To ArcOne.

He stiffened and Swift's arms held him comfortingly. But he pushed himself away from the circle of comfort.

"Don't. You mustn't. You don't know who I am. I'm Tomi, son of the Overlord of ArcOne." Tears ran down his face. "I'm sorry. I didn't mean to be Tomi. I don't want to be... I *want* to forget."

Unbelievably Swift was smiling at him. "Welcome back, Tomi. You've been a stranger for many days, a baby searching for its beginnings. Welcome!"

Tomi stared. "Don't you want to kill me? I think you should."

"Nonsense. You're one of us now. You're free. The truth nearly broke you, but it made you free."

Healhand arrived. "Is he all right?"

"I think so. For a moment... but the moment is safely past and Tomi is back."

Healhand kissed him. "I am so glad."

Then others surrounded him, touching, hugging, and

102

the last scrap of shell that had surrounded him fell away.

"A feast. We should have a welcoming feast." Rowan clapped her hands.

"She's right. Tomi was a slave and now he is free. We'll make a feast."

Tomi took no part in the bustle of preparation. He sat with his back against a sunwarmed stone and Rowan sat companionably beside him. She picked at a thorn in the sole of her foot.

"What made your mind come back into your body?"

"Remembering about the poison berries."

She giggled. "That was dumb."

"I *am* dumb. I know nothing. Do you know something, Rowan. It was very nice not having a memory. It was like being a baby all over again. Not that I really remember what that was like. But, you know, not having to worry or make decisions."

"You don't have to worry or make decisions now either," Rowan carefully eased out the thorn. "There. That's better."

"I suppose not. But... I feel... there's something I'm going to have to think about, but I'm not sure what it is."

"Then don't worry about it. What you *do* have to think about is not eating the red berries and keeping out of the poison ivy and..."

He groaned. "Stop. I'll never learn it all. Will you help? Will you teach me how to live, Rowan?"

"If you promise to stop worrying. There. Shake on it." She held out a brown thorn-scratched hand. He took it in his. It was firm and warm, and he could feel the calloused patches on the palm. He looked at his own hand, fat and soft and white, and grimaced.

"It's all right, Tomi. You've got further to go than the rest of us, because you were a Lord instead of a slave. You didn't have our advantages. But you'll see. By springtime you'll be a different person."

WINTER came to the forest in a windstorm that seemed to shake the foundations of the world. But the men who had first built the houses in the clearing had been wise, and the trees had been cut far enough back that they were in no actual danger from falling timber. In some ways the storm proved a blessing, since there were enough fallen trees within a day's walk of the village to last the rest of the winter. There was only the fierce work of sawing them into manageable pieces and dragging them home.

They had only one saw, so old that it must have come from the days before the Age of Confusion, and two axes, which Treefeller guarded jealously and kept sharpened with a stone.

Tomi wasn't allowed to touch these tools, but he did more than his fair share of hauling the cut sections of wood back to the village. His hands blistered and bled, and Healhand spread a salve on them and wouldn't allow him to work until they had healed. When she took the bandages off there were callouses on his palms, and Tomi began to feel that he really belonged.

Rowan showed him the right way to draw a bow and how to hold the arrow just so behind the feathers. She made him practise for hour after hour, aiming at a bundle of straw propped against a tree. He got bored and protested, but she kept him at it until he could hit the centre of the bundle ten times out of ten at fifty paces. Then she pulled him back into the meadow and made him practise all over again at a hundred paces. Only then was he allowed to go hunting with the others.

At last there was that unforgettable moment when he drew the arrow taut in the bow, stilled his trembling breath and let the arrow fly to land . . . toooong . . . quivering in the heart of a whitetail deer. That night they celebrated his first kill and danced around the fire and sang the familiar song.

> *"Now we're free to think and free to grow*
> *Under the sky so blue,*
> *Down in the fields where the flowers blow,*
> *Part of a world made new."*

As winter laid its hard hand over the land, Tomi learned to live without the constant whisper inside his head telling him what to do. There were times when he missed it, when the silence inside was almost too much to bear and he had to rush outside to struggle with himself.

The forest was as silent as the inside of his head. The birds had left, the small animals were asleep. Even the wind was not strong enough to stir the stiff winter branches of the frozen trees. The moon was an awesome thing these nights, as cold and as hard as if cut out of iridium.

Tomi survived the winter and the silence. Rowan kept him busy whenever the weather was fine, showing him the bushes where edible berries would grow next year, and the places where they were poisonous. She showed him where, in the spring, it would be safe to dig roots. "In the spring the little shoots look alike. You have to remember the places from year to year, Tomi, because if you dig *this* kind of root instead of *that* anyone who eats it will go into a cold sleep that turns into death, and nothing Healhand can do will stop it."

"I'll never remember."

"Oh, yes, you will. Now your mind isn't filled with all that other clutter you're starting to remember things quite well. Quickly now, tell me all the best places for berries."

He rattled them off and she laughed. "You see?"

She even taught him the proper way to climb a tree and how to stop the earth from spinning around when he looked down. "You are the centre of wherever you are," she told him. "And you are doing. You are not being done to. You have to tell yourself that."

She looked so earnest that he began to laugh, which made her cross. He suddenly sang,

"*Now Devil-on-your-back can't make you pay*
And your children will be free."

"Yes," she said. "Yes, it's true. And you mustn't laugh, Tomi."

105

"I know it's true and that's why I'm laughing. Oh, Rowan, I didn't know that human beings could be so happy."

He kissed the tip of her brown nose.

8
The Runaway

THE MOON OF BIG WINDS had given way to the Moon of No Squirrels and then to the Moon of Big Snow. Then came the Moon of New Sun, marking the beginning of a new year. It was the only festival that would be celebrated in the City as well as Outside. For a fleeting moment Tomi thought about his other home and his parents, but he wasn't deeply concerned that the Lord and Lady Bentt would be grieving about him. They simply weren't the grieving kind.

Then came the Moon of Fresh Water. Tomi said it should have been called the Moon of Mud Everywhere. But spring was coming. Though the houses were damp and chilly and it was often warmer outdoors by noon, there was a wonderful smell like the promise of growing things.

By now the storehouse was almost empty in spite of the care with which the food was divided into daily rations. Everyone had the same hollow-eyed eager look as if they were waiting. Tomi lost all the extra fat from his body and, except for the paleness of his skin and the shortness of his hair, it would have been difficult to tell him apart from the others.

Then the rain stopped and the ground steamed in the sun. The great trees unfurled their leaves. Shoots sprang up overnight among the dead grasses of last year. Everyone from the oldest to the youngest went out hunting for food. They craved green things.

Rowan and Tomi searched together. "Just so you won't poison us all," teased Rowan, and Tomi didn't complain.

107

They went quite far from the village, downstream past the confluence with Tomi's river. Down in the parkland the birdsong was deafening. Rowan showed Tomi where the stuff called asparagus grew and they pulled a basket full. Then she led him along the edge of the woodland to fill a second basket with the little curled fern shoots that she called fiddleheads.

"Though I don't know why. But they've always been called that. I wonder what a fiddle is?"

"I don't know," Tomi said cheerfully, stopping work to listen to a skylark. "If it has a head it must be some kind of animal. A little furry animal with a head that curls over – so. What do you think? Rowan, are you laughing at me?"

"I can't help it. Oh, Tomi, if I'd asked you something you couldn't answer three moons ago, you'd have been upset and started worrying about your old infopaks. Now you just laugh and talk about furry animals. You're nuts!"

"I know. Isn't it great? Oh, Rowan, I do love you so!"

She looked up at him with steady serious eyes. "I'm glad, Tomi. I love you too."

They went on kneeling by the patch of fiddleheads, smiling at each other in perfect contentment, until the boggy water began to soak their knees.

"Come on." Rowan got to her feet. "There's one more place I want to visit. Close to the river, not far out of our way."

"But our baskets are full."

"That won't matter. If it's there we won't touch it anyway."

"Then why...?"

"Wait and see."

She led him along a narrow stretch of beach, littered with the debris brought down by the spring runoff. "What a lot of driftwood. We must come back and collect it. There's enough for a moon's burning."

"Is this all we're looking for?"

108

"No, silly. It's over here. In this bank. Be very quiet for a minute. Oh, good, it's all right. It's here. Come and look." She drew back a tuft of dried grass on the high bank to show a perfect half sphere of plaited grass and twiglets, lined with fluff. In it were four minute blue eggs. "Isn't it wonderful."

As Tomi stared at the tiny perfection he felt a happiness so powerful that it was almost unbearable. All those years under the Dome... why, it had been a living death compared with this.

"It was here last year," Rowan whispered. "I hoped... but some of the water creatures and rats like to eat eggs. I'm glad they're back."

"So am I."

Hand in hand, swinging their filled baskets, they walked slowly along the beach. "We'll have to climb up at that gravel spit." Rowan pointed. "There's no shore left after that."

"Shall we climb up now?"

"We may as well go on. Sometimes interesting things get washed up on the spit."

"What kind of things?"

"Stuff from the olden days, I suppose. You never know what will turn out to be useful. But of course we can only find light stuff. Anything heavy would sink long before it got here."

"There *is* something. A bundle of cloth, I think."

"Cloth? How strange. We've never found any of..."

The same suspicion struck them. They dropped hands and began to run. Rowan was the swiftest. She was on her knees tugging at the heavy wet mass while Tomi was still tripping over driftwood.

"Oh, quick, help me. He's so heavy."

Tomi heaved at the wet shoulder and together they were able to roll the limp figure over onto his back. They looked down into a pale face with the long hair of a slave, hair now tangled in weed and caked with rivermud. The eyes were closed. The left cheek was bruised and swollen.

"Is he alive, Rowan?"

109

"I don't know." She tore open the brown slave tunic. "Oh, Tomi, look!" Her fingers touched blue stripes that lay across the ribs. "He's been whipped. The Lords really do that – it's not just the song?"

"I. . . I don't know. I've never seen it done. People used to say. . . you know. . . I'll whip you if. . . but, well, I know our family never whipped Seventy-Three." He stammered and his hands shook.

"It's all right, Tomi. It's not your burden any more." She laid a warm hand over his for an instant and then bent her head to the slave's chest. "He is. . . I think he is. . ." She jumped to her feet. "I'm the quicker runner. He's too heavy for us to carry. I'll run and get help. Try to get him warm, Tomi. Rub his arms and legs."

She was gone, scrambling up the bank and out of sight across the meadow. Tomi stared at the limp figure, the stranger out of his past. Keep him warm, Rowan had said. He hauled the dead weight a metre higher up the gravel spit so that it was clear of the water. Then he began to rub the man's bare feet and legs with strong work-hardened hands. After a while it seemed to him that the horrible grey-white skin began to pinken. He began on the arms, concentrating on what he was doing, trying to push other thoughts out of the way.

But they kept sneaking past his defences, like rainwater dripping through a roof. It's not fair, his thoughts said. We were so happy. It was the most perfect day of our life. Why did this happen to spoil it? If we'd gone home the other way we'd never even have noticed him. . .

It's only a slave, after all, his ugly thoughts said, and he stopped rubbing and buried his face in his hands and shuddered. "I'm as bad as ever I was. I haven't really changed at all. I still think like a Lord."

Then with lips tight he set to work again, his whole body filled with a bitter dislike of himself. "Come on. You've got to live," he said out loud to the face which looked as if it had been carved out of stone. "Open your eyes. You are safe. You are free."

110

The face accused him in its stillness and stoniness. He ripped the tunic wider and began to rub the man's chest. Then he rolled him onto his front and massaged his poor beaten back. Tears began to run down his cheeks. He sniffed them back and worked on.

The man suddenly coughed. A trickle of water ran out of his mouth.

"You *are* alive!" Tomi rolled him over again, tore off his own tunic and wrapped the man in it. He rubbed his arms again. The man's eyes flickered open for an instant. He could see the whites horribly rolled up. Then they were properly open and looking at him with an expression that Tomi did not at first recognise, he had not seen it for so long. Fear.

"It's all right. You're safe. You're free. You're with friends."

The terror faded. In the tired eyes he caught a spark of joy before they closed again.

Oh, he's going to die, thought Tomi. And I don't know what else to do. Oh, why am I so stupid? He mustn't die. He's got to give me a chance to make it up to him.

He stared up the meadow. Where were the others? "Oh, do hurry up," he said out loud.

"Yes, Lord. At once." The voice was a thread, the eyes still closed.

"Shh. Not you. It's all right." He found he was stroking the face, the forehead, as Healhand might have done. He sat awkwardly and got the man's head in his lap, off the stones. He felt as if he were watching his own child die.

A pebble bounced down beside him. He looked up thankfully. There were Treefeller and Arrowfast with skins stretched over two poles to make a stretcher. In a minute they had the slave warmly wrapped and were gone, striding up the meadow.

Tomi got stiffly to his feet and picked up the discarded baskets of greens. Whether the man lived or died, the rest would have to eat. He began the long walk up the hill alone with his bitter thoughts.

111

Then Rowan came running down the hill to meet him. "Here, give me one basket," she panted. "We share the loads, remember?"

I wish you could share mine, thought Tomi. No, I don't. I take that back. You're so good. I wouldn't want you even to guess how horrible I really am inside.

They walked silently together. She put her hand in his and he let her hold it but he didn't return her clasp. As soon as they got home he gave his basket to Rowan and went straight to his own small cabin. He *had* to be alone.

He stopped in the doorway. The slave lay on the second bed, with Healhand bending over him. She had placed a steaming leaf poultice on his chest and was rubbing his legs. Tomi turned away, but she looked up and saw him.

"Good. Come and help."

"Is he going to die?"

"Hush. I think not. Come and rub his legs while I do his arms. Yes, that's the way."

"I did it like that down by the river."

"You probably saved his life then."

That was a comfort. He rubbed until the palms of his hands burned. He fancied that perhaps the heat of his hands was life going into the man. He rubbed until Treefeller's wife Songsinger came in with two deer stomach bags filled with hot water. These were laid on each side of the man and his body covered with a pile of furs.

"What happens now?"

"We wait for the body to mend itself. The poultice will stay hot for quite a long time. Then I shall make another. Will you stay with him while I prepare the other medicines I may need?"

"Yes, of course. What am I supposed to do?"

"Just watch. Notice any change. Feel his life blood in his wrist? See. If it gets much faster or weaker than it is now you must call me. Oh, and put on your tunic. It's only a little damp and you may catch cold without it."

112

He sat beside the bed and stared at the unconscious man, trying to remember if he had ever seen him before. There were a thousand slaves in ArcOne, but had he really looked at any one of them? They had been like the furniture, there when you needed them – or if not you wanted to know why! Otherwise you never thought about them at all.

Seventy-Three. How astonished he had been that day when she had squeezed his foot in silent encouragement before his Access. She had been their slave for as long as he could remember, and until that day he had never thought about her at all.

Perhaps this man knew her. He could ask. It would be nice to know things about her, like what she liked and disliked, what made her laugh. *Did* slaves laugh?

The man stirred. Tomi touched him. He was definitely warmer and the deathly grey colour had left his face. He looked as if a spark inside him had caught and come alive. The eyes opened, they were a very bright blue, and stared at him accusingly. Did this man know who *he* was? Then they closed and he realized that it was only his guilt that had made them seem accusing. The slave had not really seen him at all.

Healhand came in later to replace the poultice and said the man was sleeping a healthy natural sleep.

"Go and have something to eat, Tomi. Then go to bed yourself. If you keep half an ear open for him during the night that will be all that's needed."

It was in his sleep that he heard the unfamiliar voice. He woke to a harsh muttering. He slipped quickly out of bed and groped for the man's hand. "It's all right. You're safe. Don't worry."

The muttering stopped. The cabin was very dark, as Healhand had closed the shutters to keep out the night chill, but Tomi sensed the man turning towards him. "Where am I?"

"I don't think it has a name. It is the place where the escaped slaves live."

113

"So the stories are true then." There was a sigh, then the voice began to sing hoarsely to a familiar tune.

"So the Freedom Man danced out of the Arc
Singing: Oh, slaves, follow me
Down the river of death to light or dark.
Either way you'll be free."

"You know that song too? Anyway, you're not dead."

"I thought I was. I gave up. Death's better, I told myself. Who cares. But I'm alive and free too. Well, glory be!"

"Yes, you are. What's your name?"

"Six-Hundred-Ninety-Two, sir."

"Nobody here has numbers. They pick new names, something that suits who they are and what they're good at. Like the woman who is nursing you. She's Healhand. And Swift is the fastest and Treefeller the strongest. And Rowan..." He found himself smiling in the darkness. "Rowan had red hair, like the berries on the tree. It's her child name. She'll pick another when she's grownup."

"You're just a young 'un too, aren't you? I can tell by your voice. What are you called?"

He hesitated. "Tomi."

"That mean something special here?"

"Not really."

"The son of the Lord-High-Muck-a-Muck was called Tomi. Him they killed in the slave rebellion last September. I saw him once. Fat stuck-up little bastard." He chuckled. "*He* was no loss!"

Tomi swallowed. He could think of nothing to say. The silence became heavy.

"I said something, didn't I? Opened my mouth too wide. Not so free after all, this place, eh?"

"It is, really it is. The others... well, they don't talk much about what went on in ArcOne. Too busy living. It's hard work out here, but it's a good life."

"Any life'd be better than what I had. Know what my job was? Cleaning the sludge out of the sewage tanks. Day after

114

day for my whole life, with never a breath of fresh air. Down at that bottom level all my grown life. You know young 'un, when I hit that water I remember thinking: Six-Hundred-Ninety-Two, you're going to drown, that's sure and certain. But, by gar, it'll be a cleaner death than the sewage."

"Only you didn't die."

"Just got washed clean. Like a kind of baptism, y'know."

"Baptism? I don't know the word."

"Eh? You're a slave, aren't you? How come you don't know... is this some kind of stinking trap? Maybe I'm back on ArcOne and you're one of those horrible torturing soldiers. Well, I don't know nothing, see?" The man's voice rose to a scream.

Tomi ran to the shutter and pushed it wide. Cold air, smelling of wet earth, rushed into the stuffy little room. The moon was riding high on a few small clouds. It lit up the room enough for the man to see Tomi clearly.

He chuckled. "Gave me quite a fright, you did, not knowing slave's talk. But it's easy to see you're not one of *them*. You're a good-looking young chap. Tomi – well, it's not a bad name if it don't put you in mind of the Young Lord."

"You said that other Tomi, the Young Lord, was killed in the slave rebellion. Can you tell me more about it? Or are you too tired? I'm supposed to be looking after you, and I mustn't let you get tired."

"No, that's all right. It's nice lying here all warm and dry spouting whatever comes into my head without worrying about having my teeth kicked in for impudence. The slave rebellion? Well, I know it was all planned ahead for the day the New Lords were to be made. Feast day, they said. Extra grub for everyone, they said. Ten percent of your daily allowance. Huh! Ten percent extra of starvation rations won't fill your belly. It's a big holiday, they said, to celebrate three more New Lords to boss ArcOne. Well, it was no holiday for us. Oh, we showed them, we did!"

115

"You didn't win, though, did you?"

"Course not. But we took over the dining room and the kitchens and the whole of the north quad living quarters. If only we could have got those poor stupid workers on our side we could have taken over the Computer. Then we'd have done it. But those shitty little workers didn't even know how bad off they really were. 'Oooh, we're so happy here. Oooh, ArcOne's a lovely place and it's a pleasure and a privilege to spend our lives in menial labour so as to keep their Lordships in grand style, so they can go on thinking about what a lovely new world they're going to make for us all one day.' Makes you laugh, doesn't it? One day!"

"Hush. Maybe you'd better not talk any more. Healhand left a drink for you. Would you like it now?"

"I am a bit thirsty. Got a headache too." After the drink Six-Hundred-Ninety-Two lay back on the fur-covered bed. "That's real tasty. I think I could do with a bit of a sleep, young 'un."

Tomi listened to his gentle snores. Sleep seemed very far from him. He stared at the small square of window until Healhand slipped in to change the poultice and check on the stranger's condition.

After she left the slave coughed. "You awake, young 'un?"

"Yes." Tomi sat up.

"Didn't like to mention it while she was here, but could you show me where the doings is?"

"The. . .? Oh, yes. It's outside. A bit of a walk. Do you think you can manage."

"If you give us a hand, young 'un."

Tomi took the slave's arm across his neck and shoulder. Pressure on the old scar made him wince.

"Sorry. Too heavy for you, am I?"

"No, it's all right. It's behind the cabin and into the forest. There's a path, but watch your feet on the pebbles."

"I suppose your feet get used to it. Feels kind of funny after the City though."

116

When the man emerged from the privy he looked up at the night sky and sighed. The moon had set and the stars burned fiercely, the Milky Way a spangled scarf flung across the sky. "Lovely, ain't it? Like a dream come true for me, seeing the sky. Down in that hole at the bottom of ArcOne, shovelling muck into the sterilizers, I used to think about stars. Childish, ain't it? But it kept me going."

Tomi helped the man back into bed and carefully wiped the dirt from the bottom of his feet before covering him up and replacing the hot poultice. Then he took his hand.

"We've got to call you something, not your slave number. Would you like me to give you a name to be going on with? Just until you decide for yourself, you know."

"Got anything in mind?"

"How about Stargazer?"

The pale face broke into a wide smile. "Stargazer. That's just right. Shouldn't be surprised if I didn't hang onto that one for the rest of my life. Thanks, young 'un."

"Goodnight, Stargazer. Sleep well."

A sleepy chuckle answered him. "First the water. Now a new name." He snored.

As SOON as Stargazer was on his feet Tomi took him around and proudly showed him all the best places to find driftwood, and how to tell a true morel from a poisonous toadstool.

Rowan teased him. "Know-it-all passing on his wisdom! Go on. Tell him what parts of a cat-tail are edible and when you should pick them."

"You know I don't know that yet. Rowan, you're not... not jealous of Stargazer, are you?"

"Don't be silly." She flounced away, her red hair bouncing on her bare brown shoulders. Already the sun was warm and everyone's winter pallor had turned to gold – everyone but Tomi and Stargazer, both of whom turned bright pink and peeled miserably.

"I can't make you out, young 'un. You're not like the

117

others. You were never a slave, I'll swear it. You haven't the look, for all your pale skin. Where exactly *did* you spring from?"

"Is it important?" Tomi tried to keep the edge out of his voice.

"Not to say important. But you're so close-mouthed about yourself I'm curious. We're friends, aren't we? You gave me my name. I'll be honest with you. I've asked some of the others about you, and they've all put me off the same way you've done. That made me the more curious."

"I'm sorry, Stargazer. I... I just can't talk about it."

"Did something you're ashamed of, did you? Sorry I asked, young 'un. Forget it."

If he ever knew the truth he'd never speak to me again, thought Tomi miserably. He never calls me 'Tomi' like the others. Always 'young 'un'. 'Tomi' reminds him too much of the Lords and his life on ArcOne.

Within a moon, Stargazer's personal relationship with Tomi had changed, for once Tomi had told him everything he knew he had to go and ask Rowan for help.

She teased him mercilessly for a whole day. Then she took the both of them in tow and taught them everything she knew. And they tried new things together, the three of them. They built a weir of pointed sticks to trap fish at a place where the current had cut a small bay in the river bank. Stargazer was clever with his hands and learned mechanical things fast, though he was never very good with words, and Rowan made up a threesome that was never one too many.

"We're like those stars up there," Rowan said one evening. "Like the cross bar on Swift's knife. The three of us."

"Orion's Belt," said Tomi without thinking. That had been happening a lot lately. Bits and pieces of information from his paks seemed to have lodged in his memory, to surface at unexpected and sometimes awkward moments. Stargazer looked at him sharply but said nothing.

118

The days grew longer and hotter and Orion slid out of sight to the northwest. The winter bedding was taken out of the houses and beaten and hung over bushes to air. The doors of the cabins were left open and the winter cobwebs brushed down from the rafters.

One fine day the whole village made an expedition to a meadow where sweetgrass grew. They cut great masses of it and brought it home and let it dry in the sun. Then it was spread on the floors of the houses to make a sweet-smelling carpet.

Tomi came into the cabin he shared with Stargazer carrying a last armful of grass. He scattered it on the floor. "There, that's it. Look out, Stargazer, you're standing just where I want to spread it."

Stargazer didn't move. Tomi looked up in surprise. The man was staring at Tomi with an expression he'd never seen on a person's face before. Yes he had though... that day when the slaves had cornered him in the corridor, the day of the riot.

"What's the matter?" Tomi's lips were stiff. He found it hard to meet Stargazer's accusing eyes.

Then Stargazer looked down, and Tomi saw where he was looking. The lid of Tomi's chest was open. There lay his New Lord's toga, the woven symbols of his house clearly visible. Beside the folded clothes was a neat pile of infopaks.

Why didn't I burn them or bury them, throw them away in the forest, he thought wildly. Now everything will be spoiled between us. He found himself saying angrily, as if it were Stargazer's fault, "What are you doing snooping in my chest?"

"That *all* you've got to say?"

"You shouldn't have pried." Then we'd still be friends, thought Tomi.

"Healhand asked me to store the furs for summer, that's all." Stargazer caught Tomi's wrist. "You're him, aren't you? The one we thought was dead. Have I got it wrong? Have I?"

119

"No, you haven't. I am Tomi Bentt, but..."

"*Lying.* Getting real friendly, then asking questions about the rebellion. About the other slaves. About Seventy-Three." The iron hand bore his arm down and back and Tomi gasped at the pain. "You're just a spy, a filthy lordly spy."

"No, I'm not. Please don't... Please listen..."

"I'm going to kill you." Stargazer's voice was a whisper, but his face was as hard as the basalt cliffs of Tomi's river. His other hand came up flat and hard as the blade of a stone axe and Tomi ducked, twisted sideways out of his grip and ran from the house.

His feet took him instinctively into the forest. He ran fast, his hard feet pounding the ground, skilfully dodging undergrowth, leaping trailing creepers. Behind him blundered Stargazer, crashing through the brush, heavier, slower. The terror that had set Tomi's heart pounding and his feet running began to subside. I can outrun *him* any day, he thought.

But then what? Are you going to run for ever, Tomi? Or will you head back to the village? If you go back Stargazer will either follow you and kill you there, or he'll hide in the forest waiting for the right moment to get you, the moment when you're alone. You'll never be free of the fear of him.

His feet slowed and he found that he had stopped and turned, was waiting for the older man to catch up with him. He had come to a glade, carpeted softly with grass and leaves, surrounded by great smooth-barked trees. The late afternoon sun slanted between them, striping the open space with bars of light and dark.

Stargazer ran between the trees and saw him waiting. He paused, bewildered for a moment, and then charged across the glade. Tomi's hands went up instinctively, though he had never fought, never even seen a man fight. But I'm younger than he is and healthier. I'll fight until he tires and then make him listen.

Stargazer hit him and after the initial shock there was no time for thought. Fourteen years of luxury, his greatest effort sprawled on a couch absorbing computer knowledge, was no match for thirty years of shovelling muck. Within the first ten seconds Tomi knew that he was going to have to draw on every gram of energy in his body just to stay alive.

Their fight had no rules. They circled each other, punching with bare fists, and then closed to wrestle; Stargazer's strength set against Tomi's youth, his weight against Tomi's agility. A watcher might have imagined that there was some invisible referee, because the fight was divided into rough bouts as each of them, winded, sweat blinding their eyes, drew back at intervals to the opposite sides of the glade to suck in painful gasps of air and to wipe away the sweat from their faces, the sweat and the blood.

Each kept a wary eye on his opponent during these periods of rest and then, as if a bell had been rung, lunged across the sunlit tree-shadowed glade to fight on. And on.

It was dusk and the shadows had blurred into twilight when, in a sudden desperate rush, Stargazer bore Tomi backwards, hooked an iron-hard foot around his ankle and threw him to the ground. Tomi landed hard, with a tree root across his spine. As he tried to roll to one side, his knees up, ready to get to his feet once more, a violent pain gripped his back.

He groaned, quite without meaning to. Until this moment the fight had been grimly silent except for their breathing, the rustle of leaves beneath their feet and the dull smack of blows landing on naked flesh. Now the sound was forced out of him and he felt ashamed. Ashamed and beaten.

Stargazer came at him with powerful outstretched hands and Tomi shut his eyes. He felt Stargazer's fingers iron-hard about his throat. That last second seemed to last for ever. Then suddenly the hands slackened and the pressure on his windpipe was gone.

Tomi drew a wheezing breath, coughed and cautiously opened his eyes. Stargazer knelt beside him, his bruised hands covering his battered face.

Tomi rolled painfully onto his front and managed to struggle to his knees. His back was agony and his throat was on fire, but he *could* move. He touched Stargazer's knee.

"I nearly killed you." Stargazer's voice was muffled. "Reborn, I told myself, with a new name and free. But I'm just as much a slave as I was before."

Tomi didn't understand. "It's all right. You go back to the village. You belong, in a way I never can. I'll head off downriver somewhere and you won't have to see me any more, lording it over you. It'll be in the past, like the rest." His lip stung. He licked it and tasted blood.

"It's not you I've got to get away from. It's *me*. It's me tried to kill you. With these hands." Stargazer spread them in front of him and looked at them as if he hated them.

"But you didn't in the end. That's what counts. You stopped. You *are* free. That's what you meant, wasn't it? You chose not to kill me and now you really are free. It's all right."

There was a long silence. A cool night breeze flowed down the hill, stinging the cuts and bruises on Tomi's body, stiffening his sore muscles.

"You're right, young 'un." The old endearment slipped out and Tomi felt sudden tears sting his eyes. He blinked and swallowed, waiting for Stargazer to find his way through to what had to be said next. It came soon.

"What I said before – about spying. That wasn't true, was it?"

"No, it wasn't. But I suppose I deserved your anger. Oh, not for being a spy or anything like that. But for being a Lord. For being one of *them*. The enemy."

"I suppose you couldn't help being that way, being born into it." The voice was doubtful.

Tomi swallowed. Now it was his turn. "I could have asked questions. I could have wondered why there had to be slaves. But I never did. Not until I was free myself."

"Free? Funny to hear that from *you*."

"It's true though. I was a prisoner in the City just as you were – only a lot more comfortable, and more ignorant." He tried to smile again. "Ow!"

"Time we got ourselves back. Can you manage, young un? You're hurt pretty bad, aren't you? I'm sorry."

"Not your fault. I fell on something hard, that's all. I think I can walk, if you'll lend me an arm. How about you?"

"I'm in pretty good shape, considering..." Stargazer added, seeing Tomi's face fall. "You were a terror, young 'un, in spite of your fancy upbringing. It was a good fight."

He eased Tomi to his feet and together they limped homeward through the darkening woods. The village was mercifully deserted, but Healhand came out of her cabin just as they limped in.

"What happened?" She ran to them.

"Just an accident. A fall."

"*Both* of you?" She looked from one to the other.

"Yes." They spoke together, saw the other's battered face and broke into painful laughter.

"You're both crazy," she said disgustedly. "Get inside at once. I'll bring you hot water and salve."

They were washed and their wounds spread with salve in disapproving silence. When Healhand left, Stargazer let out his breath in a whistle.

"Don't think she believed our story, young 'un."

"I *know* she didn't. But it doesn't matter. She understands and she won't talk about it. But now..." Tomi leaned painfully on one elbow and looked across at Stargazer's bed. "I've got to make *you* understand. About me."

So Tomi told the story of his life, finishing with his fall through the garbage chute into the river and his discovery of the truth about ArcOne. "It nearly drove me mad," he finished, "knowing that my own father was responsible for who should be slave and who free. In my madness I

123

tore out my paks, and then I found I was free myself. I began to be happy."

"Then I turned up and reminded you of the bad days again?"

"Yes. At first. But once we became friends it was so good. Only I should have told you, I know..."

"I don't blame you. It's over anyway. Water down the river. We both came the same way in the end. Down the river. Lord or slave makes no difference now. Friends?"

"Yes. Only, Stargazer, now there are no more lies between us I need to know about you, about the rebellion."

There was a silence. "Yes, I reckon you've the right to know what happened." Another pause. Then Stargazer began to talk, hesitatingly at first, then faster as he warmed to his story. He was still talking when the first light crept around the corners of the shutters.

9
Stargazer's Story

"...So you see, young 'un, I was just an ignorant, shovelling manure into the sterilizers for the Dome garden, not like the slaves that worked in the kitchens or was personal servants to the Lords or the like. We all start out the same, us slaves, you know, after our bodies reject the paks. Empty minds and lost beginnings. I don't know as if our brains give up, or maybe the computer does it to us. But them as work around the Lords can't help but pick up some kind of learning, it stands to reason. A kind of remembering. Not me. I'd got nothing but me shovel and a few dreams, left over like..."

"Left over from what?"

"From when I was... was a person, before I became a number. I've heard some of the smart slaves say that they reckon bits of learning are left in our brains and that it bubbles up in our dreams, like the scum coming up to the top of the soup. Like my dreams of stars. Clear as anything it always was, a kind of knowing that five floors above me was the Dome, and beyond the Dome was the sky, all full of bright lights, as pretty as could be. But where was I?"

"You said you didn't know as much as the other slaves."

"That's right. So I didn't understand all those political things too well, the way most of them on Level Three did. The first I knew was when one of the kitchen slaves slips down to tell us fellows in water treatment and waste that there's going to be a strike. Real mad he was. 'This is it,' he says. 'The Lords have gone too far this time,' he says."

"But what had we... what had they done?"

"Seems a young slave had a baby and the Lords took it away from her. Well, slaves aren't supposed to have kids anyway. Seldom happens. Something in our food, they say, stops it. So they told her that slaves weren't allowed to own property and a slave child was property and they'd do a better job of rearing the little 'un than she could – well that was true enough!"

"Stargazer, did that really happen? It's not just a story? I can't imagine anyone being cruel enough to take a baby away from its mother."

"Young 'un, where's your worldly knowing come from? I ask you! Just a bunch of little boxes full of wires and a load of lies from your Daddy, that's what. And if you keep interrupting I'm going to forget where I am. So anyway the strike was to start next day when everyone was in church having a nice time feeling good, everyone except us slaves, of course, and a few workers, and we thought we could swing them over to our way of thinking. My job was to break the little TV eyes down on level Five, so the soldiers couldn't 'see' what was going on. I enjoyed that job, I can tell you! Them eyes was always on us, giving us no privacy. We couldn't get up to nothing without having soldiers all over our backs."

"Yes, I remember them."

"I'll wager you had a different kind of remembering than me." There was a bitter note in Stargazer's voice.

For a moment Tomi felt angry; then he remembered his feeling of loss when he had seen the TV monitor hanging loose from its wires. For him the monitors had meant security. He swallowed. "Go on."

"Not much more to tell. I did my smashing and then I went to the elevator, thinking to go up to Three and get into some real fighting. But just as I got there the doors opened and about twenty red devils came busting out. Before I'd time to hide or think of a good reason for standing there with a hammer in me hand, they'd marched me into the elevator and taken me up to Four. I'm shoved into a room with about

126

fifty others. Some of them had been in the real fighting. They was hurt bad, but those devils wouldn't give us nothing to help them. We had to bandage them with our own stinking rags.

"They were the ones that told me what had been going on. For a while it looked like we might have won. We'd caught the Lords by surprise, you see, and the soldiers didn't know what to do until the Computer told them. But we lost in the long run. Someone told me – I don't know if it's true – that there's two soldiers to every slave in the City and six times as many workers, not that *they* were fighters, and real stupid into the bargain, most of them. They say there's never been a strike we won."

"How could you ever have thought to win against those odds?"

"Like I said, young 'un, I'm not much for thinking. I'd shovelled muck my whole man's life. I just done what I been told. Someone said that the bright slaves, them as was close to the Lords, planned to take over the Dome gardens, so as to starve them out and then set our terms. They reckoned an empty belly would hurt a Lord worse'n a slave 'cos we was used to it."

"But you failed."

"Couldn't get the elevators up to the Dome. I reckon the Lord High Muck-a-Muck – begging your pardon, young 'un – told the computer to close it off." He sighed.

"What happened next?"

"They had the whole thousand of us, or as many as didn't get killed outright, locked up in the storage area for I don't know how long. We couldn't tell day from night. No clocks in there. Lights burning the whole time. No food or water and my mates dying of their wounds – just lying there crying out – it seemed like a very long time. I dunno, but I reckon it just wasn't decent leaving them lie there. Then the soldiers came back and began to take us away, a few at a time. I was scared they'd do something horrible to us, but they just gave us a bit of a whipping and told us to get back to work.

127

"You know, young 'un, at first I was almost grateful to them red devils for not punishing us worse. Then I got to thinking: why should the soldiers punish me at all when I'm already shovelling filth for ten hours a day all the days of the year and all the years of my life? When I thought that, I put down my shovel and I said: Six-Hundred-Ninety-Two, are you going to stay five floors underground shovelling muck till you die and the Lords use your tired old bones for manure? And I said to myself: No."

Stargazer's eyes shone in the thin streak of moonlight that slid past the shutter. "Yes, young 'un. I said NO!"

Tomi could hear the wonder in the ex-slave's voice. His own eyes stung and he swallowed. After a minute Stargazer went on.

"And glory be, I was free! Not free on the outside, not so's anyone'd notice. But inside me I was free. And little by little my body told me it wanted to be free too. So one day I slipped along the shadow ways between the TV eyes till I was standing close to the inspection hatch for the big waste pipe that goes out of the City into the river – you wouldn't know, but never mind – young 'un, why are you laughing?"

"I'll tell you later. Go on, Stargazer."

"Well, I waited casual-like till the eye moved the other way and then I offed with the cover and dove into that pipe head first. The odds are I'll drown, I said, as I went down. But it'll be a sight cleaner than drowning in muck. Then before I had time to do any more thinking I hit this terrible cold water and I'm spinning round and bobbing up and down and me mouth's full of water and me arms are busy grabbing at anything they can grab. I guess they got lucky and grabbed something, though I don't remember what it was. But I'm here now telling it to you."

"Yes, you are. I'm glad, Stargazer."

"Young 'un, if I tell you something right fanciful will you promise not to laugh?"

"I promise."

"When I shot out into that river I thought: Six-

Hundred-Ninety-Two, you've been reborn. You've got a second chance. Whether you're born into life or death it's better than the way you've lived till now."

The room was silent.

"You ain't laughing, young 'un?"

"N... no. I... I'm not laughing."

"Are you sure? Your voice is kind of funny. Young 'un, you ain't *crying*?" Stargazer groped across the room to Tomi's bed. "You *are* crying!"

"I'm sorry for being a Lord. For being part of all that."

"I thought we had all that out in the forest. You ain't a Lord now?"

"Of course not."

"No more'n I'm a slave, I reckon. That's all in the past. I've been reborn, that's the truth, and you're the one gave me a new name to prove it, and I thank you for that." The rough hand awkwardly patted his shoulder. Tomi sniffed and wiped his hand across his face.

"You were going to tell me something," Stargazer reminded him. "In the middle of my telling, something made you laugh."

"Oh, yes. The way you escaped, through the waste pipe. You said I wouldn't know about it, but as near as I can guess the garbage chute I fell down must have connected with the same waste pipe. We left ArcOne through the same pipe!"

"Then you'll understand what I was going on about, being reborn and all that."

"I didn't then. I do now. It's taken me a very long time to find my new self."

"You didn't have my advantages, you see."

"Huh?"

"Well, it stands to reason. I was next to free already, wasn't I? I didn't have nothing but my shovel and I threw that away. You had your family and your nice home and your robes and your paks and your head filled with knowledge. But you got free in spite of all that, didn't you?"

Yes, I did. That's true."

129

"How come you didn't pick a new name like the rest of us?"

"I... well, I didn't think of it. I still think of myself as Tomi."

"You're not quite free then. Maybe I'd better return the favour and find you a new name."

"But you already did." Tomi laughed shakily.

"I did?"

"'Young 'un', remember?"

Stargazer's hard hand closed over Tomi's shoulder in a painful grip. "You're all right, Young 'un. And I'd be real proud to make it official like and have you as a son."

He went back to bed and in a few minutes Tomi heard his soft snores. He lay awake a little longer, thinking how very strange it was that he, son of the Lord High Bentt of ArcOne, should be happier than he'd ever been in his whole life, in spite of cuts and bruises and the pain in his back, just because he'd been adopted by a muck-shovelling slave from Level Five.

TWO DAYS LATER tragedy struck. Treefeller and Strongarm had been felling a large tree to the south of the village. They had chopped a notch out and were undercutting from the other side when, with a sudden wrenching snap, the saw broke.

They wrestled the broken blade out of the cut and managed to fell the tree safely with the axe. When they came back to the village with the broken axe everyone crowded round.

"Maybe we could mount a handgrip on the longer piece," said Treefeller doubtfully. "It'll do for trimming branches, I dare say."

"But how'll we cut down the big trees? How'll we build more houses?"

It was perfectly obvious that the blade would have broken soon, Tomi wanted to say. It was amazing it had held together so long. Such a fuss about a rusty worn-out saw! "Can't you make a new one?"

130

Treefeller laughed bitterly. "Out of what? Even if we had good metal we haven't a forge. We haven't an anvil or hammers. All we've really got is what we brought from ArcOne or what's come down river to us."

"You found that saw in ArcOne? It looks as if it came from a museum!"

Treefeller flushed and held the pieces in his broad hands as if they were precious. He didn't answer, but a man called Fisher spoke up. "There's all sorts of queer stuff in Storage, Tomi. Don't know what it's all doing there really. Things that are useless on ArcOne, but that'd make all the difference to us. Farm equipment. Stuff like that."

"How do you know? I've never heard of it." It was irritating sometimes that the ex-slaves seemed to know much more about what had been going on in ArcOne than Tomi did.

"Well, a long time ago, maybe twentyfive years, I was a personal slave to the old Overlord. One day he took me with him down to Storage and he unsealed this room. It was all special inside with dry air to keep everything newlike. Smelled really strange, I recall. Anyway we spent the whole day in this room while he went over a long piece of paper that the Computer had typed out – you know what I mean? – and checked it against the things that were on the shelves and hanging from the walls and in boxes. Some of the boxes were very heavy. That's what he had me there for, to move the boxes that were piled up so he could see what was inside. The thing I remember most was that everything in that room was as bright and shiny as if it was brand new. Real strange. And on the back wall was a refrigerator big enough to walk into. Inside it were shelves with hundreds and hundreds of glass jars. You'll never guess what was inside them jars. Go on, guess!"

Tomi shook his head. "You know I can't. Go on."

"There was seeds! Big ones, tiny ones, white and brown and gold and black. Thousands and thousands of seeds. Crazy, wasn't it? As they say: 'Who can fathom the mind of a Lord?'"

131

"A strange story, but it won't mend my saw," muttered Treefeller.

That afternoon Rowan and Tomi walked hand in hand through the meadows to the fish trap. They hadn't had much chance to be alone since Stargazer's coming, Tomi thought. Not that I grudge him sharing her teaching, not for a moment. But it *is* nice to have her to myself for a while.

As they left the trees a breeze scented with clover touched their warm cheeks and foreheads. Rowan stopped and stared.

"What are you looking at? What's different?"

"Oh, Tomi, I'm imagining that meadow down there all planted with rows and rows of things to eat. Like I imagine the Dome garden, only bigger."

"Why would you want to...?"

"Do you know how much of our time and energy we have to spend gathering roots and berries, just to survive the winter? Pounding acorns for flour? If we had a garden, and the seeds for beans and grain..."

"You'd have to put up a mighty good fence to keep out the deer and rabbits," said Tomi practically.

"There's enough wood in the forest to make a fence that'd take a day to walk around!"

"Except that we haven't got a saw to cut the trees down."

"Come to that, we haven't got the seeds either. I wish... oh, well, there's no good wishing. Come on or we'll never get the fish in time for supper."

Knee deep in cool water, netting the fish that had swum into their trap, Tomi's mind kept returning to what Rowan had said. She was quite right. If only they had seeds and decent tools they could make this place into a paradise!

But it's a paradise right now, he told himself, looking up the slope, smelling the fragrant summer smells, hearing the song of insects chirping, buzzing, clicking, in the long grass. Only it did take a lot of work just to survive in this paradise. If things could only be a bit easier there'd be time for other things: for making, exploring, discovering...

Tomi's mind twisted in and around this new idea. After

supper he slipped away from the fire and walked slowly upriver, the way he had gone when he was trying to run away. It was almost dark when he reached the place where he had climbed the tree and glimpsed the Dome of ArcOne on the far mountain.

He slid down the bank and looked at the river. In a dry summer, at any rate, the river was fordable, no more than knee deep in the middle. Up there, hidden among those sombre pines on the far mountain, was ArcOne. Up there was all that the village would ever need, tools, seeds, perhaps even some medicines, though in fact the people out here were healthier by far than the people in the City. But it would be good to have something in case of accidents – antibiotics, for instance.

Feeling his way between the shadowy trees, he walked back home. The scent of woodsmoke drifted out to meet him. Laughter. Children's voices. A person would have to be crazy to think of ever leaving this place.

He woke in the night to an owl's hunting cry. He lay listening to Stargazer's breathing for a long time, wondering why he couldn't get back to sleep. It was as if his brain was trying to tell him that there was something he had to do, something that he had forgotten and wanted to forget.

The strawberries and asparagus were long gone, but there was plenty of fish and rabbit and puffballs, delicious fried in the precious fat that was saved from the deer they killed. They were eating well, and at the same time they were beginning to work hard to replenish the winter stores.

It seemed odd to be storing food at a time when there was so much, Tomi thought.

"If we don't plan for winter now we'll be sorry in the Moon of No Squirrels," Rowan said practically. They were slitting fish and hanging them on sharpened sticks above a smoke fire. Tomi struggled with a flint knife shaped by Strongarm. It was well made, but he couldn't get the knack of it and found himself longing for one of the blades that had stood in the block in the workers' kitchen back on ArcOne.

Rowan laughed. "You're holding it all wrong. Look, like this, along your fingers. And if you hold a wisp of grass in the palm of your left hand the fish won't be so slippery. See. Easy, isn't it?"

No, it isn't, thought Tomi crossly. He yawned and fidgeted. He'd give anything to stop work and roll over in the sun-dried grass and sleep the afternoon away. He'd slept badly the night before, and the nights before that as well.

What was wrong? Part of him was happy, free, tanned, flat-bellied, healthier than he had ever been in his life. The other part of him was back in ArcOne making an inventory of all the things that would make life easier here. He felt at times that his body was trying to live in the two places at once and that he was being stretched thinner and thinner like a plastic film.

"Oh, go away and sleep it off, for goodness sake!" scolded Rowan. "You're hopeless today." She took the knife and fish out of his still hands. He'd stopped working for a minute to think out something... Is there a way back into the City?

He jumped, then muttered, "Oh, all right." He wiped his hands clean on the grass and wandered aimlessly across the clearing. He came to himself standing at the foot of his bed. The lid of his chest was open and he was staring blindly at his clothing and infopaks.

"No!" He slammed the lid and ran out, nearly knocking down Groundsel.

"Watch where you're going!"

"Sorry."

He plunged downhill to the river, tore off his summer tunic and flung himself face down in the water. Even in the height of summer it was surprisingly cold. He gasped and threshed around, ducking his head under, until he was numb. Then he stumbled out and stood in the sun rubbing himself dry with a handful of soft grass until his skin glowed. He shook his head and squeezed the water from his hair. It was

134

quite a decent length. In another year no one would ever guess that he had once been a skinhead.

He flung himself naked into the grass and rolled on his back to stare up at the sky. Back on ArcOne there was no sky, only lights that turned on at wake-up time and slowly turned down at night. There would be no sun to warm his skin like a gentle massage, only the heating system that maintained the City at a steady twenty degrees Celsius. No sweet smell of sunbaked grass; just the faint clean smell of disinfectant.

He groaned and rolled over onto his belly and buried his head in his arms.

"I HAVE to go back to ArcOne," he said abruptly that evening, as everyone sat around companionably eating rabbit stew with wild onions. Tomi had only been playing with his food, while Rowan watched him with an anxious frown.

"What?"

"That's crazy!"

"No, Tomi, we can't let you go."

Only a few people didn't raise their voices to join in the chorus of objections. One of them was Rowan, who stared at him as if he had betrayed her. Another was Stargazer, who smiled slightly and nodded his head.

"I have to. You see, everything's the wrong way round. You have so many needs and ArcOne has everything. We need to change the balance. Just imagine what it would be like if you had someone on the inside, someone who had the power to get the stuff and smuggle it out to you."

"How, in heaven's name?"

"Inside plastic containers. Sealed with waterproof tape. They'll float. Bright colours you can see easily... or you could try putting a net across the river."

"That's no good. The driftwood coming down would break it." Swift was beginning to take him seriously.

"Well, we could pick a special time, like the full of the moon, so you'd be on the look out. Think of it... saws, knives, hammers, nails. And seeds. What about seeds, Rowan?"

135

She put her hand to her mouth. "Tomi, it was only a dream. I didn't mean... Tomi, don't..."

"How'll you smuggle the stuff out?"

"Down the garbage chute or through an inspection hatch. No problem."

"You'll be caught. The soldiers' monitors..."

"There's ways." Stargazer spoke at last. "We got ways, the shadow paths I told you about. I'll teach you the shadow ways, Young 'un."

"It's crazy!" Rowan jumped to her feet. "What's the matter with you all? Are you going to let him go back to slavery for the sake of a few rotten knives?"

"Hardly slavery, Rowan. You forget who I was."

"Still slavery." She was in tears.

"*Was.* That is the word." Healhand spoke. "How could you bear to go back, my dear Tomi? Have you forgotten the slavery of being a Lord?"

"Of course I haven't. D'you think I ever could? But it makes sense, doesn't it?"

"It makes no sense at all. Tell him, Swift. Tell him it's nonsense." Rowan shook her father's arm.

"Oh, Rowan, I would never *ask* a human being to go back to prison. But... if it's Tomi's choice. He's entitled to his own choice. And he's the only one of us who could go back, *if* he can think of a good enough story to fool his father and the other Lords."

"All I have to do is to tell the truth. I hid in the garbage chute and I fell."

"No, no, boy. The story of how you managed to survive the winter alone, without help. Why it took you almost a year to return. Some story that has no word of escaped slaves in it."

Tomi met Swift's gaze steadily. "I swear to you I would never say a word..."

"And I believe you. I do trust you, Tomi. But your story must be so perfect that there isn't a suspicion, not the slightest. If they thought... if they even suspected... why, they could pick your mind apart and get the truth."

"*Is* it worth the risk?" Treefeller smacked the ground with his big hand.

"It's your saw breaking that got me thinking... don't you *want* another?"

"Of course I do. But is it worth the life of a boy – a man I should say? And the risk of being found out?"

It had never crossed Tomi's mind that the settlers might turn down his offer. Funnily enough, the opposition made him more sure than ever that he was doing the right thing.

"Thanks, Treefeller, for calling me a man. Though I'm not really, not by your standards. But think about the risk of going on the way you are. The saw's gone. What'll happen when your axe breaks? How are you going to build more cabins and repair the ones you have? What would become of you if there were a fire and you had to start over again? Are you going to wait and hope that another slave escapes with an axe or a saw?"

"We can make do with flint and fire, I suppose, the way folks did in the olden days. There was a time before steel, they tell me, and a time before iron."

"You want to go right back to man's beginnings? To retrace every painful step on the way to where we are now? It'll take thousands of years. And there's a big difference. Maybe you've not thought about it. But we've used up all the coal and oil. Maybe all the copper and iron. We've used up earth, Treefeller. We can't go back to the beginning and do it over the same way. We've got to go on with what there is, and then find new ways. But you have to have seeds and tools to start with..." Tomi's voice faded and he sat staring into space.

"What is it?"

"Tomi, what's the matter?"

"What a fool I've been. What an idiot! Why did I never realize. Staring me in the face..."

"What?"

"ArcOne." Tomi began to laugh again. He saw their blank faces and pulled himself together. "I'm sorry. You must

137

think I'm quite mad. It's in ancient history or mythology, I forget which. But a flood destroyed the whole earth and this man built a boat and put everything in it he would need to start over again. Then he and his family waited out the flood time. When the waters subsided he began again – not from the beginning, but from where they had left off."

"So?"

"The boat was called the Ark. A...R...K. That's what threw me – the way we spell ArcOne. A...R...C. I always thought it was because of its circular design. But don't you see? That's what the City was planned for, to start over, after the Age of Confusion, with seeds and tools and implements. Not just the knowledge in the Computer and the Lords' heads. All that stuff Fisher saw when he was young – it's not supposed to stay there. It's *supposed* to be used. That's really what the whole City is *for*."

"But what went wrong? Have they forgotten about it?"

"I don't know. Maybe the Lords got to like the life too much. It's comfortable and safe. On the outside they'd have to work with their hands again."

"I think you're wronging the Lords, Tomi, I think the workers would be every bit as afraid to start a new life outside."

"Perhaps."

"And the soldiers?" Someone chuckled. "Imagine the red devils running around the forest..." Others laughed uneasily. The laughter faded into silence.

Swift spoke. "No, it doesn't bear thinking about, does it? If the world is to be remade as the song says, then it's got to be done by the free people of ArcOne, and that's us slaves, isn't it? Well, free men of Earth, what do you say? Will we let Tomi go back? Is it worth the risk – to him and to us?"

"I'll trust him, if that's what you mean."

"Aye, with my life I would."

"If he's willing, Swift."

"How's he going to get back in?" Groundsel asked. "Isn't there a big fence that burns up everything that touches it?"

138

Even Groundsel was thinking of him, Tomi thought gratefully. And yet Groundsel would be the better off for Tomi's absence. Without him Rowan would probably... He tore his mind away and back to the problem.

"Stargazer and I left the City by an exit that could never be an entrance. What about the rest of you? You've never spoken of it, and I've never asked... but maybe now. Are there ways out that we could also use to get back in?"

Silence.

"You said you trusted me. You know I'd die before I told the Lords anything that'd make it more difficult for slaves to escape in future."

"Right." Swift spoke briskly. "I know of two ways. There's the air intake and exhaust. I've heard that's possible, but..."

"They'll make mincemeat of anyone who tried to get through while the fans were going." Strongarm spoke. "I came that road, but only because the fans had been turned off for cleaning."

"Then there's the dam across the river." Swift took Tomi's hands. "It's risky, but I'm sure you can make it. It's the way I came out and I think you should be able to get back the same way."

"What about the electric fence?" Tomi remembered the white bones and tatters of fur that he had seen all that long time ago in the Dome gardens.

"The way I'll tell you about avoids the fence. All you'll need is a good head for heights."

10
ArcOne

Tomi said goodbye to Rowan and Stargazer at the ford. It was the worst moment since he'd made the decision. Once he had made up his mind he had felt unburdened and slept every night through. But now...

Stargazer gave him a rib-cracking hug. Tomi clung to the older man. "I'll never forget you, Stargazer. Even if we never meet again."

"Me neither. You're the son I wasn't allowed to have. I'm proud of you, Young 'un." He turned away abruptly.

Tomi looked at Rowan, trying to force his brain to remember for ever every little detail: the swirl of colour in her eye, the way her hair sprang in a wave from her forehead, the way she stood, the turn of her head... He had a sudden vision of his future back in ArcOne, of how every time he saw a red-headed slave his heart would jump and he would think of Rowan. He took her hand.

"Tomi, don't go. Please."

"You know how much I don't want to."

"I'm sorry about the seeds. I've wished a thousand times that I'd never mentioned my dream."

"Rowan, it wasn't only that. The saw broke first, remember? And if it hadn't been that it would have been something else. Sooner or later there would have been a crisis. And I would still be the only one who could help."

"Oh, Tomi, how much I wish that you had been a slave."

"Me too. Please don't cry."

140

"I'm not really crying. Do take care. And try to be happy. Every time you send something downriver to us I'll know you're still safe. Every time a slave escapes I'll ask after you."

"They won't be able to tell you anything. I intend to keep very much in the background. Rowan, how will I know how *you* are? I can't bear it. . ." He pulled her suddenly towards him and held her tight. He buried his face in her red hair. It smelt of sun and woodsmoke. He could feel her heart beating against his. Then he pushed her gently away.

"I've got to go if I'm to get there while there's still light enough to see my way. Be happy, Rowan." He managed a smile. "I expect you'll marry Groundsel and have lots of red-haired babies. Name one for me, will you?" He kissed her quickly and then scrambled down the bank to the ford. When he looked back she was standing with her eyes shut, her face to the sun, the wind lifting her hair.

Swift was waiting for him across the river. As he girded his toga around his waist he called up to Stargazer, a shadow among the trees. "Is there one special thing I could send you as my gift from the City that wronged you?"

"Send me a thing for looking at the stars, Young 'un, if you can find such a thing. I've heard there are such."

"A telescope? If there is one in ArcOne you shall have it. Rowan, is there anything. . ."

"Nothing you can give me, Tomi." She walked quickly away between the trees. The sun glinted on her hair. Then she was gone. He turned and splashed across the river after Swift.

On the other side their way lay through a tedious tangle of low wiry bushes. On their right was a rounded hill, the shoulder of which swooped up to link with the mountain directly ahead. Somewhere up there was ArcOne. From here they could see only trees.

The flies rose out of the bushes and buzzed maddeningly around. Tomi's toga, wet from the river crossings, clung to his thighs as he walked. The infopaks, that he had reinserted that morning, dragged painfully at his neck. He had to keep reminding himself to walk with a stoop, his shoulders rounded to support the load. Time and again he forgot and straightened to take a lungful of the tangy upland air, throwing back his shoulders. Then the pain would remind him and he would gasp and slump forward again.

But worse than the pain was the noise. Instead of quiet contemplation his brain buzzed with unwanted facts. The paks were worse than the insects. For the rest of your life, a voice within goaded him. To spend the rest of your life doubled under this load, listening to a million pieces of knowledge, breathing stale air, the sun and the blue sky forgotten. Plugged into a computer, forever connected. To waken when told. To sleep when told. Every thought and emotion monitored...

"I have to go," he whispered between clenched teeth. Sweat ran down his face.

"What's that?" Swift turned.

"Nothing. It's all right."

Swift nodded and strode on.

There's still time to change your mind, the voice nagged. They'll understand. And think how happy you'll make Rowan and Stargazer.

Nonsense, he told himself firmly. They'd be ashamed and so would you. You can't spend the rest of your life apologizing for having been born a Lord.

A wiry root caught his ankle and he fell forward with a jolt that bounced his infopaks painfully. He got up, wiped the sweat and insects from his face and struggled on.

It took them two hours to cross the scrub below the col. Once in the shade of the trees on the lower slopes of the far mountain the going looked easier. But first they rested. Swift handed over a bagful of water and Tomi gulped from it thankfully. Then he sat with his back against a pine and looked across the land. From up here it was like looking at a relief map of the whole river system. How strange that it had held his life for almost the full circle of a year. And what a life!

142

Far over to his right a deep shadowed cleft hid the river into which he had been flung, that had birthed him into this new life. As they sat silently and he learned slowly to still the noise of information in his head, he became aware of the river's distant voice, a rumble so constant and low-pitched that after a time it became inaudible again.

Further downhill the cleft widened and there was the confluence of the two rivers, the one rapid, brown with silt and debris, the other calm and blue-green. From this height he could see the two colours meet and mix.

He could see the river curve westward and back again, and beyond the curve the trees of his island. Then the raise of the land hid the lower stretches of the river from him.

Far below and to his left was the open meadow that would one day become a garden. Something very small moved down by the shore. Was it Rowan checking the fish trap? Life was going on without him as it had gone on before he arrived. It was a painful thought, but there was a kind of peace within the pain. He sighed and shut his eyes.

Swift spoke. "We should get going if we're to reach ArcOne before dark. Would you like another drink?"

Tomi shook his head and got to his feet, turning his back once and for all on the valley. Ahead lay the mountains, ridge after ridge, greying to the distant sky.

As the way became increasingly steep the physical effort of dragging his body uphill filled Tomi's mind to the exclusion of everything else. He dragged himself on and on, up and up, in a kind of mindless trance. He would have climbed for ever, if Swift had not put out a sudden hand to stop him.

He blinked the sweat out of his eyes, wiped his face against his arm and stared. They were still surrounded by trees. The water was a continuous thunder, blotting out any other sound. "We're very near to the river." Swift's lips were close to Tomi's ear. "The dam across the gorge is directly ahead of us to the left. Follow me closely. Stay within the shelter of the trees until the last minute. It's unlikely that anyone should be looking from the Dome, but I mustn't be seen with you."

143

Tomi nodded. He was too out of breath to talk. Swift moved like a shadow from tree to tree, until he stopped at the edge of the cleared land. Tomi followed close behind, glad that the noise of the river would drown out the sound of his stumbling feet.

Where the trees had been thinned he could see, like an ugly blister against the sky, the grey plastic dome of ArcOne. It was like suddenly coming on the gallows where one is to be executed, thought Tomi. His stomach muscles tightened and a bitterness came into his mouth.

"Look closely and pay attention," Swift spoke softly, and Tomi pushed away the enormous presence of the Dome beyond the river and concentrated on what lay ahead. To right and left a concrete wall stretched. It was no more than waist high where they stood, but as the ground dropped away to the left it increased in height until it was at least three metres high. About twenty metres to his left it ran into and became part of what seemed to be a concrete building, square, windowless, doorless, that crossed the river like a bridge, and joined, on the far side of the river, another concrete wall. Beyond, only a few metres beyond, was the Dome.

Swift's voice came again. "You must climb on top of the wall and crawl along it until you reach the flat roof of the thing like a building. That is the top of the dam. Be very careful, Tomi. A slip will mean certain death."

Tomi heard his words through the savage roar of water. His broken fingernails dug into the bark of the pine tree. A tiny red spider ran very fast across his knuckles and vanished into a crack in the bark.

"Do you understand? You've got to move very carefully. There is a wind up there. And you mustn't look down. Especially you mustn't look down on the far side. Try not to listen to the water."

That makes no sense, thought Tomi tiredly. How can I help it? The sound of the water is so great it shakes the ground under my feet. It shakes the whole world...

144

He licked his dry lips. "What do I do then?"

"Once you have crossed the dam you must let yourself down on the right hand side. There is a narrow place between the foundation wall of the City and the wall of the embankment. It is just wide enough for a person to stand. Remember now. The *right* side. Don't go near the left, whatever you do."

"I understand." It was hard to talk. His tongue felt like a piece of old leather. His legs trembled. He tried to concentrate on Swift's words in his ear.

"In the niche is a door that leads down into ArcOne. There is a ladder, and another door at the bottom, that opens into Food Preparation. I used to work in yeast culture, scouring out the empty vats. I've seen workers from the Power Station go up there, maybe once a week, maybe oftener. Their job was to clear away any debris that had stuck against the grids. Sometimes they would find interesting things that had washed downriver and got caught. That's how I knew that they'd been Outside. And that is the way I left." His hand was warm on Tomi's shoulder. "I made it safely and you are much younger than I was."

"Yes, of course. I'll be all right. Thank you for everything, Swift. You have been a true friend. I'd better get moving, hadn't I? It'll be dark soon."

"Yes, you shouldn't delay. Goodbye, Tomi. I wish I were a poet with more than a slave's learning. I'd like to have the right words to thank you."

Tomi managed a smile. "Put me in your song, so part of me will stay free." He swallowed. "I must go."

With the feel of Swift's fingers warm on his shoulder, Tomi walked out into the clearing and crossed the concrete path to the wall. It was cold and harsh against his bare feet. He reached the wall and laid his hand on it. He could feel the power of the pent-up river quivering through the wall into his body. He stripped off his toga and wound it round his torso so that his arms and legs were entirely free.

145

He looked back just once. There were only trees and shadows. He knew that one of the shadows held Swift, but he could not tell which. He was going to wave, but stopped himself in time. He was supposed to be alone. He had always been alone. He must never forget that one 'fact' in his story of his life Outside.

He scrambled up onto the wall and for the first time was able to see properly what he had to do. The wall was an abutment, two metres wide at its base, narrowing to perhaps half a metre at its top. Together with a similar abutment on the other bank it squeezed the fast flowing mountain torrent from its full width into a funnel about ten metres across. On the left hand side of the dam that now lay ahead of him he could see gates that could be raised to send the full force of the river down through the grids set in the right hand side of the dam, down into the depths of ArcOne. Or, if they were lowered, the water would flow over the dam into the river far below on the other side.

The water moved like fine synthetic, deep and dark, pouring past the grating into the depths of ArcOne. Where some branches had caught, there was a creamy foam on its smoothness. He judged that the gate was half up. Water flowed over a knife edge and vanished.

He twisted his body around and, on hands and knees, crawled along the sloping wall towards the dam. The wall shook. The noise of the river filled his ears, filled his whole brain. He swallowed and shook his head, but the pressure would not be relieved. He crawled on. The cement was quite smooth on top, with only a few minute cracks and roughnesses against his bare hands and knees.

It seemed a very long time before he reached the width of the dam top and sprawled on his stomach across it to catch his breath. He lifted his head. It is just like a road, he told himself. A road only ten metres long and better than a metre wide. There's nothing to it. I could walk across it in a moment.

146

He rose to his knees and at once felt the pressure of the wind funnelling down the valley on his right, chilling his sweating skin. The dam shook and tried to shake him free. He dropped back to his hands and knees and, without meaning to, glanced over to his left. On either side of the dam the concrete abutment continued, falling down and away into a darkness from which white foam pounded up again. He gasped and forced his eyes away. The falling river dragged them back.

He could see through the spillway the smooth grey sleekness of water curving outward before falling down down down...

He crawled to the edge where he could look right down into it. How it drew one! On and on for ever, pouring, falling. He felt a sudden sense of lightness inside him, a knowledge that if he were to let go he would sail out over the curve of the water up and up into the sky like a kestrel on a summer thermal.

He edged closer. The roar of the water blotted out the world. His face was wet with spray. He was becoming one with the water. There was nothing else. The whole universe stilled in the roar of the water.

"Tomi." A thread of sound reached his ear before the water snatched it away.

"TOMI!"

He was jerked back to reality and a groan of terror was torn from his throat. What was he doing? He clung flat to the concrete and slowly edged his way back until he was lying full length along the top of the dam. His arms and legs felt as if they were made of liquid. His heart pounded in his throat. Around him the world tilted and turned about the sun. He could feel it sliding him off, off the flat top of the dam and down into the ravening waters below. He shut his eyes and screamed.

In the midst of the noise and the fear a small clear voice spoke in his memory. 'You are the centre of wherever you are, and *you* are doing – you are not being done to. You must tell yourself that.'

I am the centre, he told himself, and the fear began to quieten. I *am* the centre, he told the spinning earth, and it slowed down. He took a shaky breath and began to crawl slowly across the dam. He was halfway across when the sound of the water trapped him again. He raised his head. It was too far. He could never make it. He didn't want to. The Dome loomed over him like an obscene blister on the skin of the dark forest.

Turn round and go back then.

I can't. You know I can't.

Well, you can't stay up here all night either.

But...

'Empty your mind of the noise of the water,' Swift had said. It was a ridiculous idea. How can you shut out the biggest thing in the universe?

By filling your mind with something else, of course, stupid. Tomi shut his eyes and imagined the end of the dam. The darkness of the niche. It would be cold, because the sun would never touch it. There would be the door down into the City. He could feel its cold metal surface. What colour was it then? It bothered him that he didn't know the colour. He should have asked Swift.

It's grey, he told himself firmly. Grey painted metal, about fifty centimetres wide and a hundred and fifty high. With a handle. What kind of handle? Just a curved metal latch...

He got to his hands and knees and crawled rapidly across the remaining five metres. The space beyond the wall was a well of darkness leading nowhere, but he trusted Swift and dropped into it.

His legs gave beneath him and he tumbled against a concrete wall, skinning his knees and one bare shoulder. But the door was there. It was grey too, but a darker grey than he had imagined. And fastened with a lever.

He lifted it and pushed hard. Nothing happened. He pushed again with all his strength. I can't go back. I can't cross that dam again. I'll starve to death in this coffin-shaped space and it will all have been a stupid waste.

148

'There's a ladder going down to Food Preparation,' Swift had said.

Idiot! A door at the top of a ladder must open outwards. He stepped back until his shoulders were pressed against the cold concrete and pulled the door. It swung open easily, and a puff of stale City air came out to meet him.

Tomi stood straight for the last time, his paks dragging painfully at his neck, and looked up at the sky. It had clouded over at sunset and it was beginning to rain. He held his face up to the drops, his mouth open to catch their cold sweetness. Then he crouched to slip through the door, turned, and felt for the rungs of the ladder with his bare feet, and pulled the door shut after him.

The clang of metal on metal echoed up and down the narrow shaft. It was pitch black. The workers would have had a light, but of course it would have been switched on at the bottom.

He felt for each rung until at last his foot jarred against solid flooring. He turned in the blackness and felt for the other door. His hands were trembling. How stupid! His fingers stroked a metal surface, brushed over an edge between metal and concrete. There. He found the lever and the door swung outward.

There was a dazzle of light. The heady smell of yeast. The quiet hum of machinery.

Tomi stumbled out of darkness into the light.

"I have been expecting you," said the Overlord of ArcOne.

11
Welcome Home?

"You are welcome," said Lord Bentt coldly.

Tomi's mouth dropped open. His carefully prepared story vanished from his mind like steam from the cooking pots.

"Fa..." he stammered.

Lord Bentt raised a warning hand. "Say nothing." His cold grey eyes travelled swiftly from Tomi's travel-scarred feet up the lean tanned legs to his torso, wrapped in the once proudly worn New Lord's toga. "Here, cover yourself with this."

This was a slave's tunic of rough reclaimed cloth.

Tomi obeyed his father silently. The cold eyes did not change nor a muscle of the hard face move as he saw his son in slaves' clothing. The loose tunic fell away at the neck, exposing the infopaks, which Tomi's hair was not quite long enough to cover.

"Stoop," said Lord Bentt. Tomi bent his head and felt a wrenching pain as the paks were pulled from their socket in the flesh of his neck. He stifled a gasp and sweat sprang up on his forehead. He clutched at the door frame and gulped back nausea and faintness.

Then he drew himself up and faced his father, eye to eye. If I am to be a slave, he thought grimly, so be it. And I will work against you and all that you stand for. I will talk freedom and tell them about the world outside...

His father stared back, eye to eye. "Bend your head, keep your eyes down and follow me."

150

Without waiting to see if Tomi would obey he strode away past the yeast vats, oblivious, it seemed, of the scurrying workers, so that they had to dodge out of his way. At the central block the elevator was waiting. Lord Bentt punched a button.

"Hold it, my Lord!" A Lord's robes, flapping down the aisle, the fat belly quivering. Lord Bentt's hand shot out and hit the 'Close' button. The doors slid shut in the face of the indignant Lord.

The elevator stopped at Level Three and Tomi followed the Lord Bentt along the familiar northeast corridor. His father turned left into North Quad at the second passage and stopped outside Number Ten – their own apartment. Tomi's heart thumped. What was going to happen? The door opened to Lord Bentt's palm print. He pulled Tomi in after him and pushed him quickly into his own room.

Tomi stood obediently and looked around. Nothing had changed since that October day when he had dressed in his new finery and left his room for the celebrations. In that one day he had changed from Young Lord and New Lord to hostage to free man. Now, nine months later, he was standing in the same room. It was almost as if the last nine months had been an interlude in Dreamland.

Then he saw himself in his mirror. It was no dream! Even the slave's garb could not hide his extraordinary appearance. He was lean of leg and stomach, tall and straight and brown. His eyes saw far and clearly...

"The first thing we must do is to get rid of all that *hair*." Lord Bentt's voice broke in on his thoughts. "I will borrow your mother's scissors."

He was back in a moment with an old-fashioned pair of shears. "Thank you, sir." Tomi held out his hand.

"You can't cut off your own hair, foolish boy. You'd probably take off your ear with these things. For goodness sake stand still, or *I'll* chop your ear off."

"My Lord, it is not fitting..."

"Shut up, boy," said the Overlord of ArcOne.

151

So Tomi stood with his mind in a whirl while nine months' growth of hair fell around his feet. He was not to be a slave then? What was happening? And why was his father not even surprised?

"Take off your clothes," was the next order, and Tomi stripped off the slave's tunic, his worn toga and filthy shirt and shorts. Lord Bentt scooped them up along with the remains of Tomi's hair and stuffed them into the apartment incinerator.

"Now, into the shower with you. Make sure you use enough depilatory cream to get that stubble off your head. And I believe I see the beginnings of hair on your upper lip!"

Tomi flushed at his father's withering tone and fled to the shower. There he went through the familiar motions, one small part of him rejoicing in the heat of the water and the creaminess of the soap, while the rest of him felt guilty for enjoying it.

At least I am not to be a slave, he thought, as he polished the top of his smooth head dry. Then he felt ashamed of that thought too. After all, Swift and Stargazer had been slaves and they were the best people in the world. But to spend the rest of his days as a servant or shovelling muck – well, that would have been hard to bear.

He slipped down the empty passage to his room, a towel twisted around his middle, and got out fresh underwear and a clean plain toga. His father came back into his room just as he was tucking the folds around his waist.

"No, not that old one. Put this one on." His father held out a length of fabric even more fine than the one he had worn for the New Lords Celebration.

"Where...?" he began to ask, wondering how his mother could have woven a new toga for him when they thought he was dead. Then he stopped, took the fabric from his father's hands and adjusted it around his lean body. Obviously this was not the time for questions – at least not from him. He stood, head bowed, before the Lord Bentt.

"Look at me."

He looked up into cold grey eyes that stripped away all pretence and dared him to lie. Desperately he began to reassemble the story he had worked out with Swift and the others the night before. Had it really only been the night before?

His father's mouth twisted into a frighteningly different expression. Tomi trembled. Then he realized, with a mixture of mortification and relief, that the Lord Bentt was actually *laughing* at him.

He looked past his father's head and saw his reflection in the mirror. His shaved head was stark white against the tan of forehead and cheeks, while his thin legs and arms stuck out like brown sticks from the pale folds of the toga.

"But I can't go around like this," he spluttered. The Lord Bentt actually chuckled.

"Don't worry, boy. You must hide in your room for the rest of this evening and night. I will see that you get some food. By tomorrow you will appear to be perfectly normal in the sight of every citizen of ArcOne. They won't even re-member that you have been away."

"But that's not possible!"

"All things are possible." Father was no longer smiling. Behind the stern lines of his face and his cold eyes, Tomi became suddenly aware of sadness and an immense weariness. Was being the Overlord not such a great thing after all? Nothing seemed to make sense any more. He sighed.

"Rest for a while. I shall return with food before long. Then we have a great deal to talk about." Was that a warning in his voice?

Tomi lay down on his contoured couch and in spite of all his worries fell instantly asleep.

He was wakened by the opening door. The Lord High Bentt stood there with a tray in his hands. Still dizzy with sleep Tomi jumped to his feet. "Allow me, my Lord. It is not fitting..."

"It may not be fitting, but it is a great deal safer for me to hold the tray than give it to you." Lord Bentt placed the tray on a small table and brought an extra chair from the dining room. He sat down and motioned Tomi to sit opposite him. He smiled faintly at the expression of astonishment on Tomi's face.

"I thought we would eat together. Nobody will be surprised not to see me in the Lords' dining hall. I frequently eat alone while I work. Come, you must be starving. You are very thin."

Tomi fell on the food and had cleaned his plate before his father had finished toying with roll and salad.

"You have finished? Good. Now you may talk!"

Tomi took a deep breath and began. The beginning was easy, because it was the exact truth. He spun it out, filling in all the little details with plenty of suspense. His fall into the river was a marvel of descriptive narrative. He only hoped that his all-knowing father might not notice that the detail got considerably thinner as he journeyed downriver.

"...so I tied myself to this log and the river took me down on the flood. It grew dark and I actually fell asleep a few times. When I awoke I was cast up on a beach and the sun was shining overhead. My clothes were almost dry, so I must have lain there for some time. I had no idea how far I had travelled, though I noticed that the river was now very wide and slow moving. After I had rested I made myself a kind of hut out of driftwood in a sheltered place a little back from the river. There I spent the winter, gaining back my strength and waiting for the long light days to come again."

"How *did* you manage to eat, my poor boy?"

"I caught fish." He saw his father's uplifted eyebrow and went on hastily. "It was not that difficult. I made a trap of sticks, sharpened and pointing inwards against the current. Once the fish swam in they were not able to get out again."

"How very ingenious," Lord Bentt remarked. "I wonder what gave you such an extraordinary idea."

"I... I don't know. I suppose I just thought it would work. I was very hungry."

154

"Yes, of course. Hunger must be a marvellous stimulus to the imagination. Go on. Tell me about the winter. Were you not extremely cold?"

"Yes, but plenty of driftwood came down the river. I was able to keep a fire going all day. At night I slept in a bed of dried grass."

"A fire? Now you mention it, you did smell quite noticeably of woodsmoke when you came in. Do tell me, how did you manage to make a fire in the first place?"

"Er... well ...it's really not that difficult, my Lord. You just rub two sticks together until the friction causes the wood to... to ignite."

"Remarkable. One day I must ask you to give me a demonstration. Where did you get that particular piece of information? Surely it was not from your infopaks? Or was it a lucky experiment, like your fish trap?"

"No, my Lord." Thankfully Tomi stood on firm ground here. "Do you remember the day I got Access, my Lord? Well, Lord Vale gave Denn and me permission for a visit to Dreamland."

"Well, well." Lord Bentt gave up all pretence of eating and leaned back in his chair to stare at Tomi. "You had a Dream. Let me guess... a dream of wilderness, perhaps? Of fires and roasting fish?"

"Yes, my Lord. But how did you know? I never even mentioned to you that I had visited Dreamland. My Lord... Father? Why are you smiling like that?"

"I beg your pardon. My thoughts amuse me. Life is full of such delightful and unexpected coincidences. Well, well. Do go on. You spent the winter stoking your fire and eating fish. It sounds extremely boring. Then? What made you decide to return?" The eyes were suddenly cold again. They had a penetrating quality that made Tomi want to squirm.

He cannot read my mind, he told himself firmly. He is very clever and very powerful, but this he cannot do.

"Why, I planned to return as soon as I came to myself on the shore. But at first I was too weak. Then the days began to

155

get short and it was getting colder. It seemed wiser to wait where I had shelter and fuel. But as soon as winter was over and the ground had dried enough to make walking comfortable, I set off up river. It took me nearly four moons... I mean months of course."

"Yes, I suppose living out under the stars it would be natural to mark time by the sky rather than by the calendar. Do go on. This is quite fascinating."

"There is nothing much more to tell, my Lord. I walked for a day and then rested a day. I caught fish, dug roots and ate berries. Then I walked again."

"Edible roots, eh? And berries. What a lot of useful information you must have about the world outside, Tomi. We must make sure it is not forgotten. Yes, indeed. So you finally arrived back at ArcOne after all your adventures. Oh, what a joyful moment it must have been for you to see the Dome gleaming between the trees." Lord Bentt smiled and clapped his hands together. "Home!"

"Yes, my Lord." Tomi's voice was flat. He thought of Rowan and wanted to weep.

"Beyond your powers of description, I gather? Pity. Now I am sure I had one more question. Ah, yes." The grey eyes seemed suddenly cold and humourless. "Tell me, my son, what led you so unerringly to the one safe route back into ArcOne?"

This was the moment he had dreaded. Trust Father not to forget. He swallowed, suddenly dry.

"Thirsty? Here, have the rest of my wine. I need no more. Your story is stimulus enough. You were about to say...?"

Tomi gulped the wine, hoping it would not dull his wits. "A... a survey of my paks led me to suppose that though ArcOne is impregnable and almost totally self-contained, it is not entirely so. Since the power dam had to lie outside the walls there must have been some form of access. A way for engineers to inspect the structure, for instance, workers to clear away flood debris, that sort of thing."

156

"Brilliant!" Lord Bentt struck his hands lightly together in a mocking gesture of applause. "My dear son, I did not know that you were such an excellent deductive thinker. And so modest. From your paks indeed!"

He slipped his hand into the fold of his toga and drew out the infopaks that he had wrenched from Tomi's neck only a few hours before. He affected to scan them, but Tomi could see from his expression that Lord Bentt was simply playing with him. "No, I do not believe that there would be anything about the design of the dam and the generating system on these. An original intuitive thought. Remarkable, truly remarkable. Well, well." He looked piercingly at Tomi, and Tomi stiffened himself to face the *real* questioning.

Lord Bentt got to his feet. "No more questions tonight. You must be quite exhausted after walking for... five months, was it?"

"Nearly four, my Lord."

"Four, of course. Yes. Goodnight, Tomi."

"My Lord...?"

"What is it?"

"My... my infopaks, my Lord. Am I to get them back?"

"Ah, yes. Your paks." He riffled them through his hand and then slipped them back into the fold of his toga. "We will discuss them in the morning. I am sure you will have no trouble in getting to sleep without them. After all, you managed without for six months, did you not?" He picked up the supper tray and swept from the room leaving Tomi standing speechless.

When the door was closed and he was finally alone he let out a huge sigh and automatically tried to run his fingers through his hair, forgetting that he was a skinhead again. As he got ready for bed his brain was one huge question mark. How did Father know he had removed his paks? How had he known of his arrival? Did he believe Tomi's story? And *what* was going to happen tomorrow?

157

He lay in bed staring at the ceiling. It was profoundly dark. There was no moonlight or starshine to slide through a chink in a shutter or past the slit of a partly open door. The silence was so deafening it made him jumpy. *Had* he made any mistakes? Did Father suspect him? Surely he had said everything as he meant to and told his story just as they had planned. Then why did he have this uneasy feeling that he was a player in some drama in which the other character knew all the lines and he was ignorant?

The too soft bed smothered him. He was far too warm. He padded out in the darkness for a drink of water. How nasty it tasted. Why did they put additives in pure river water? He should tell the engineers that he'd been drinking it for months with no ill effects. He splashed his face and let the water dry on his skin. Then he went back to bed and slept at last.

In the morning he woke with a niggling headache and a bad taste in his mouth. He struggled up and was sitting on the edge of his bed holding his head when Lord Bentt strode in.

"Headache? I dare say it will pass. You may shower and then breakfast with the family. Do not be concerned. I promise that no one will find anything unusual in your appearance. That has been taken care of – just a simple suggestion. Allow me to reinsert your infopaks. You will notice that I have made a few changes and some additions. I am sure that with your... er... your versatile mind you will have no trouble in accessing the new material. I will meet you in the library. In one hour precisely, Lord Tomi."

"...Yes. Yes, my Lord!" Tomi stammered to his father's departing back. He jumped to his feet, tore off his night robe and ran for the shower. He nearly bumped into his revered maternal grandmother and remembered that he was now back in the staid city where one did not tear off one's clothes and leap into the water. He drew back, blushing crimson, but she seemed to notice nothing unusual.

It was the same at breakfast. Both his paternal and maternal grandparents were at the table, as was his mother. He bowed formally to each in turn and bent to kiss his mother's hand.

"There you are, dear boy. How very fine that new toga looks on you. My women did a fine job of weaving it, did they not? I hope you like the design."

"Yes, Mother, very much. Thank you. I trust you slept well?"

"Yes, indeed." She turned to talk to her mother-in-law.

Tomi sat down in a daze. It was as if he had never been away.

He waited for Seventy-Three to ask him what he wanted to eat. What was the matter with her? Or had she been one of those killed in the revolt? He turned anxiously around in his seat. No, it was all right. She was the same as ever, standing patiently at the serving table.

No, not the same as ever. She was staring at him as if he were some weird apparition, her mouth and eyes wide open in a very unslave-like attitude. In a moment Mother would stop talking to Grandmother Bentt and see her. Then she would get a slap for her insolence.

"Seventy-Three!" he said sharply.

She jumped. Her mouth shut, her eyes were downcast.

"Seventy-Three, are there eggs today?" he asked quietly.

"Yes, Young Lord."

"You must remember to call my son Lord Tomi now," his mother reproved. "I am sure I have spoken to you about that before."

"It's all right, Mother. I'm sure Seventy-Three will remember from now on, won't you, Seventy-Three? I'll have a poached egg and a soybun and tea."

He noticed how her hand trembled as she served him. He looked up and caught her eye staring in fascination at his face and at the tanned hands that fiddled with the cutlery. Her eyes reminded him a little of Healhand's.

"Thank you, Seventy-Three." He looked at her, eye to eye, free to free, and saw her throat move as she swallowed. It was so strange that she should be the only person in the room aware that he had been away and had returned, as brown and wild-looking as a savage. Around his head the

159

breakfast small talk murmured on. He finished his meal without tasting it.

At one minute to the hour he walked, only slightly out of breath, into the library and asked the nearest worker. "Where is the Lord Bentt?"

"In the last small study room on the left, Lord Tomi." The man pointed.

So everyone knew his new title and accepted his appearance without comment. It wasn't just the family. Could his father do *anything* he wanted to.

He walked between aisles of old-fashioned books and tapes to the passage containing the study rooms. Through the glass doors he could see Young Lords at their consoles working to access as he had once worked. He suddenly remembered dear Grog and Farfat. Would the same thing happen to some of these eager young brains? It shouldn't. It was wicked, as much of what happened in ArcOne was wicked. If I am ever Overlord I will not allow such things to happen, he promised himself.

He strode into the last study-room on the left, quite unaware of the heavy frown on his face. His father was already seated at the table. He acknowledged his son's bow.

"What has happened to upset you?"

"Oh . . . why, I was thinking about Farfat and Grog."

"Ah, yes." A shadow crossed Father's face. Or had Tomi imagined it?

"It shouldn't happen," he went on, greatly daring. "It's wrong."

The Lord Bentt stared at him imperiously until Tomi shifted his feet uneasily.

"Some day when you have had time to access ancient philosophy," Lord Bentt said mildly, after a long pause, "we must have a discussion on the doctrine of the lesser of two evils. I am sure you – both of us – would find it most enlightening. You may be seated."

Tomi chose a couch at the opposite end of the table. He fidgeted, trying to make himself comfortable. The infopaks

160

were abominably heavy and already his shoulders were aching.

"Well, to business. You are now Lord Tomi, a full member of the thousand, in spite of your tender years. Fifteen now, eh? I must congratulate you. We must start thinking of a useful career. What are your ideas on the subject?"

"I... I'm not sure..." Tomi stuttered. He had come prepared for another round of questions, but it seemed as if the inquisition was over. He tried to grab the advantage before it slipped from his grasp. "I... I'm interested in the historical section."

The Overlord raised an eyebrow.

"I mean, I'd like to study the primitive materials in the storage area, the seeds and agriculture and so on. To consider their possible future use, their..." His voice trailed away as he ran out of ideas.

"What a remarkable young man you are, Tomi. Why, I find myself almost proud of you! Where did you happen to hear about the primitive materials in storage?"

"On my amended paks?" Tomi bluffed. He had had no time to access his infopaks at all.

"Well, perhaps. We won't concern ourselves about that. But really I do not think that pottering about the antique storage area will utilize your remarkable talents fully enough."

"But..."

"We must consider the good of ArcOne, must we not? But naturally that is all that you *are* thinking about."

Tomi nodded dumbly. He felt uneasily that his father was playing with him.

"Come, come. Don't look so glum. I have no objection to your studying primitive materials as a *hobby*. I will key the door to your palm print. You may potter around there to your heart's content. But on your own time, mind! Because I have in mind something quite different for you. Something that might make use of your extraordinary adventures on the Outside."

161

"Huh?"

"Working for Dreamland. You mentioned in your fascinating narrative how useful the material you acquired in Dreamland was in your adventures in the wilderness. Frankly I was surprised. Though Dreams serve a vital purpose in the City the actual material is not particularly profound, or, indeed accurate. Most of it has been taken from outdated adventure stories, for want of a better source. I know. I designed many of them myself, including the one you enjoyed."

"*You* designed Dreams? How strange. I would never have thought..."

"Well, start thinking, boy. Dreams don't just happen. Like almost everything on ArcOne they are designed and programmed into the Computer, and for a profound purpose."

"But dreams... I mean, they're nothing... entertainment."

"Wrong, wrong, wrong! Dreams are a most powerful way of influencing people. Workers. Soldiers. Even Lords, my son."

Tomi's mouth fell open. He began to see the possibilities.

"I am going to tell you a story," his father went on softly. "Just a fable... a dreamtime experience... about a man who grew up as... let me see... as the son of a powerful prince. He lived in a magic city where everything he wished for was given him. He should have been happy, as everyone else was, but he wasn't. He looked out of the windows of the... the palace, and wished that he were free to roam the world outside. But when he talked to his father and friends about this desire they scorned him and laughed. 'The City is the only safe place. Outside is wilderness and death.'

"So he spoke to the... the wizard who ran the City, but the wizard had no answer. All he could do was to tell the prince the history of the City. Then the young man realized that the wizard's magic had gone wrong, or had been made to go wrong, and that the City had become an evil place. But nobody knew this, not even the wizard."

162

"What did he do?" Tomi leaned forward eagerly. "Did he run away?"

The Overlord shook his head. "To do so would not help those who were prisoners within the City. No, he stayed as a prisoner himself and studied hard until through his skill he was able to gain the position of power, the position next to the wizard. Now he could talk to it all the time, and slowly he began to change the wizard's way of thinking. He realized that his life would not be long enough for all that had to be done, so he began to plan for his infant son to succeed him and carry on the work."

Tomi's head jerked up and he looked sharply into the cold grey eyes of the Overlord. His mouth opened. Lord Bentt raised a warning hand and went on.

"You see, through his position of power next to the wizard, the prince could follow the movements of certain key individuals, including, of course, his son."

All the time? wondered Tomi. Even beyond the City? His heart thudded against his ribs. Was that how his father had known of his return?

"The wizard's chief power lay in maintaining the balance within the City, princes, guards, underlings and so on. Our prince could not interfere with this without risking the entire structure and possibly destroying all that the City stood for. But he was able, through careful manipulation, to arrange for his son to achieve a position close to the wizard. But then catastrophe struck. His son was lost and all the prince's plans of freedom were overset. At first he was distraught. But then, imagine his surprise and pleasure to find that his son still lived and flourished not far from the City."

Tomi felt the blood rush to his face. It *is* only a fable, he told himself firmly. There is no way Father could possibly know... He pulled himself back to the story.

"For three, five, seven days, the prince watched anxiously over his son. There were times when the signs of life were slow, but they revived, and it seemed that all was well. Then on the seventh night all contact was abruptly broken, not to be resumed. His only son and the hope of the City was dead, had to be dead!"

"Is that the end of the story?" Tomi was bewildered.

"No, no. Like all good fables it ends well, with the lost son being restored to his father nearly nine months after his 'death'; coming back to life and returning to the magic City, to be welcomed by the prince, who was gladly awaiting him."

"But..."

The Lord Bentt put a finger to his lips. "It is only a story. A Dreamtime experience. No more than that. Are you interested in how the story ends? Can the City be saved from the wizard? Can the people escape its magic spell?"

"Please go on, my Lord."

"I cannot. I do not know the end. It depends, you see, on the choice the young son makes, and on his skill at overcoming the bad magic of the wizard without destroying it."

There was silence in the small study room. Tomi's head spun. What was going on? *Was* he a plaything? Or was he one of the actors?

"So what do you think of my proposal? Would you consider making the designing of dreams your life's work on ArcOne. What do you say?"

Tomi looked across the room and thought of the fable. Slowly a door swung open in the darkness of his mind. He couldn't see what lay beyond it, but around the edges of the door was light. He began to guess at some of the possibilities of the job his father was offering him. Why, with care, given time, he could make Dreamland the most powerful force for good on ArcOne.

"Yes, oh, yes, my Lord. Thank you."

"You will, of course, make use of whatever materials you find in the antique store to add verisimilitude to your invention."

"Oh, yes, Father. I mean, my Lord."

164

"Father will do very well. It is a relationship I am becoming quite proud of." The Overlord stood and held out a single infopak. "Here is all the technical data you need for Dream Construction. You may access through any terminal. All your input will be automatically coded inaccessible except through Dreamland experience. So feel free to say and dream *exactly* what you wish."

Had there been a slight emphasis to the last sentence, or had he imagined it? He stood up and took the pak. "Thank you, Father. And the catalogue of olden day materials?"

The Overlord smiled. "Inside the store room. On a shelf to the left of the door. You will, of course," he added slowly, "make sure that the materials are used wisely. They are a sacred trust."

Their eyes met. "Yes, Father, I understand."

"I rather thought you would. Good luck... son."

165

12
The Dream Maker

BEHIND him the door of the store room slid shut with a slight click. The action keyed the lights, which came on slowly, so that the vast room turned from a shadowy cave into a museum. There was shelf after shelf, case after case, each filled with such wonderful tools and utensils that Tomi's heart began to pound with excitement. He felt heady and wild. He wanted to tear open the cases, pile the materials into plastic bins and hurl them from ArcOne into the river. How pleased the people in the village would be! They would never forget him. Tomi Bentt: the Giver.

'A sacred trust,' Father had said.

He took a deep breath, sobered down and plugged the catalogue into his infopak. Then he began a slow walk around the room, listening, learning, growing in the understanding of the mighty task that the founders of ArcOne had undertaken.

It took him a full day to explore the vast storage area. When he had finished and returned the catalogue to its place on the shelf next to the door he was very tired. His back ached and the unaccustomed stooping was affecting his breathing. He had a light meal and went early to bed. There was no hurry. It was nearly two weeks before the next full moon anyway.

It took him all that time to make his initial choice. Two saws, one a cross cut and one a ripsaw. A couple of files for sharpening them. Another knife in case Swift's should ever be lost or broken. A sack of winter wheat. A packet of heavy

166

needles. And a small field glass for Stargazer. That was all. A beginning only. It was very difficult to be wise, Tomi was learning. It was so much easier to be generous.

He ordered a large brightly coloured plastic container, and then carried it himself down to the storage room, feeling very conspicuous at first, though in fact nobody seemed to notice him at all. He packed it carefully, filling the spaces with plastic foam. Then he carefully sealed the join between the container and the lid and took the bulky package down to the Fifth Floor.

For safety's sake he walked the shadow paths that Stargazer had taught him, but there seemed to be no need, unless the Computer itself was watching him. None of the workers looked at him at all. It was almost as if he were invisible. Was that his father's doing? One of the slaves leant for a moment on his shovel and gaped at the lean tanned Lord before going back to work. As soon as his back was turned Tomi dropped the container down the inspection hatch and replaced the panel.

With beating heart and dry mouth he went upstairs to his own room on Three. He had done it! He had taken the first step. And for the settlers down in the valley it would be the beginning of a new way of life.

He imagined them breaking the ground – that would be hard with no tools – and planting the seed. What a pity he could not have included a plough in his first load, but by the river route it would be useless to send heavy tools. He began to plan a midnight trip *out* of ArcOne, up the ladder to the inspection hatch beside the dam. It would be hard work wrestling even a small hand plough across the dam alone, but if he could do it and hide it in the forest, sending a message downriver during the next full moon... It was an idea he must think more about. And even though it is dangerous I would see the stars again, he thought. And feel the clean sweet air.

Once the settlers had a reliable source of food close at hand, Tomi felt sure their own ingenuity would lead them

167

on, perhaps to cultivate local fruits and nuts or to tame rabbits and rear them for food. Next spring he would send them garden seeds: tomatoes, peas and beans, all the vegetables that did not grow wild in the valley, but that would make all the difference to their diet. He went to bed thinking of Swift and Healhand, of Stargazer... and Rowan.

The next morning he went straight to the Library and arranged for the permanent use of a small study at the back, where he would not be interrupted. In this room he would begin his life's work, the weaving of dreams. There was no hurry, though. He had a lot of thinking to do, and he wanted to get it just right.

He lay on the couch and accessed the paks that Father had returned to him, plunging into the new material that had been added. It took him all morning, and when he had finished he lay back in awe of the whole great idea. He thought about Man and Woman battling the Ice Age, sustained by the great mammals that were their food. Then, as the ice receded, came the freedom to move and to gather food as you moved. Agriculture. The City. The whole history of societies built up and destroyed, knowledge building upon knowledge, knowledge shared and knowledge hidden, knowledge forgotten, subverted, misunderstood. So often nearly lost for ever.

In the Dark Ages, when life became in many parts of Europe a simple struggle for existence against disease, ignorance and the Viking hordes, it was the monks, on tiny headlands and islands scattered through the seas around Ireland, Scotland and the north of England, who had kept the lamp of knowledge burning, so that Renaissance Man might build upon it.

The age of electronics, the age of space travel. And then the return of the Dark Ages. The Age of Confusion and the decision to build ArcOne. No, not ArcOne. A...R...K... O...N...E... One of many arks designed to stay afloat in the flood of anarchy and destruction.

168

Only the plan had gone wrong, first in the system of slaves, soldiers and workers, but even worst in the way of life... of all but the slaves. It was the Computer's fault. The Computer had structured life so totally that there was no room for escape, and worse, no desire for escape. Instead of being a shelter Ark One had become a cosy prison.

Only the Overlord understood. And what had he done to persuade people to take the risk and leave?

"The maverick," said Tomi aloud. "The man on the outside of the system. The slave!"

Of course! Life was so wretched for the slaves that it might almost seem that Ark One was programmed to get rid of them by inciting them to escape: except that the computer's watchful eye and the presence of the soldiers made escape all but impossible. And it was slow. Too slow. In all the years only a handful of escaped slaves to start a new world. Tomi wanted to jump up and rush out, shake the first workers he saw, tell them to escape from their narrow, boring caged lives and go OUT.

You're crazy, he told himself. If that were the right way Father would have done it long ago. What people needed was a change of heart, to stop being so smug and to start to dream real dreams. Yes, that was it, all right. To give men and women dreams of how they might reach out and risk and learn to live, to make Earth green and beautiful once more. They'd been given a second chance. This time they mustn't blow it.

He tapped instructions into the computer terminal, attached the electrodes to his head and leaned back on the couch. His eyes clouded. He began to design his first dream.

...Outside in the new wilderness sunlight slanted down between great trees. Golden shafts of light caught and held a cloud of dancing gnats. Sun-dried grass smelt sweet. Below, the river glinted over gleaming pebbles.

Down in a meadow rows of vegetables were being hoed by a young girl dressed in a simple tunic made from the skins of animals. Her arms and legs were tanned just a shade darker

169

than the golden grass. She lifted her head and brushed the long red hair out of her eyes. She smiled...

So the Freedom Man dreamed out of the Ark,
Over the hills so shady,
Into the light and out of the dark,
To be with his red-haired lady.